AVAILABLE

Equestrian Fiction by Barbara Morgenroth

~ BITTERSWEET FARM 12 ~

AVAILABLE

Barbara Morgenroth

DashingBooks

Bittersweet Farm 12: Available © 2016
Barbara Morgenroth
http://barbaramorgenroth.com

ISBN: 978-0692632994

Cover photo by Diane Hadsall
Published by DashingBooks
Text set in Adobe Garamond

JULY

1

IN THE EVENING, when I returned to the carriage house after planning the Fourth of July party with Greer and Jules, I found Lockie at the desk doing paperwork.

"Hi."

"Hi." He looked up and smiled.

I realized I hadn't seen him since breakfast. "Haven't you done enough business for one day?"

"It's not business." He wrote something then put down his pen. "When I was in the hospital, a nurse gave me this journal to help me remember. It's a habit now, and good for charting training progress. I was just writing about the session on Henry this afternoon."

I stepped closer and looked over his shoulder. "Do you say uncomplimentary things about CB?"

"No."

"Is it like a diary? Private?"

"No." He closed the journal and offered it to me.

I shook my head.

"If you're interested, I have nothing to hide."

"It's from the time of your accident?"

"Yes, when I couldn't remember anything from one day to the next."

"You must have had thoughts you wouldn't want to share."

"My arm's getting tired holding it out to you," Lockie said. "I thought we were sharing our lives. This is part of my life." He placed the journal on the desk. "If you're reluctant, that's fine."

"It's not fine, is it?"

Lockie stood up and shrugged.

"Everyone has something, some incident they regret," I said.

"I do, but it's not in there." He headed for the stairs. "Dibs on the shower."

Nodding, I looked at the journal, not sure what I would find but certain he was offering it to me for a reason.

I sat in the desk chair and began read. After the first entry, I realized it was much worse than I had imagined. Knowing, in broad strokes, what had happened, didn't

2

prepare me for this. Page after page, until reaching the day he arrived here at the farm, then I couldn't go any farther.

"Tal, I've been waiting for you upstairs."

I hadn't heard him come down to the first floor and turned.

"Why are you crying?"

"I was horrible to you. I'm ashamed and sorry."

"When was this?"

"The first day." Fortunately, there were tissues within reach and I grabbed a few. "The sour sister." I pressed the tissues to my eyes. "I was. After all you'd been through. Driving from Kentucky must have been so difficult and then to come up to the house, only to have me say you wouldn't last. You needed the job and I was cruel."

I remembered that day very clearly.

Lockie took my hand. "No."

"My mother would have been so disappointed in me. I am."

"Come upstairs, take your shower, and lay down beside me."

"So we can watch professional wrestling together?" I stood next to him.

"No, I expect you'll be apologizing for the next two hours. Of course, I'll fall asleep after the first fifteen minutes."

"Did you think I was awful?"

"Did I write that?"

"I didn't get to day two."

"Did I say I thought you were the most beautiful girl I had ever seen?"

"No, you said very pretty."

"I meant more but I didn't have words."

We started up the stairs. "What does that have to do with me being rude and hurtful? Pretty girls can get away with being uncivilized? Is that why you didn't come to the house for dinner that first day?"

"You have a good memory. It's no wonder why I need you."

"Lockie!"

"What?"

"Get a digital recorder if you need a way to remember things. I'll get one for you."

"I didn't come to dinner because I was throwing up most of the evening."

"I feel worse!" I sunk onto the bed.

"Think how I felt."

"I am!"

Smiling, Lockie sat next to me. "It's a year ago. Every day since you have been wonderful, kind, and generous. Every day since, I've felt grateful to know you and to be able to live here. Even with—"

"The ugliest couch in the world," I finished.

"That, too. Look at this beautiful house to call my own."

"It is yours," I insisted.

"If that's true, it's because of you. Don't live in the past. I can't, I can barely remember it."

"How are you able to make it seem like such an unimportant part of your life?"

He took my hand. "That's not true, it's a very important part because without the accident, I wouldn't be here and this is the most important part of my life." Lockie kissed me. "Go take your shower because you have until midnight to finish your apology and then never mention it again."

I untied my paddock boots. "Who said you could make the rules?"

"Who said you could? Let it go. Of the two of us, you're the only one who cares."

"Okay." I stood. "What about Kitty?"

Lockie lay against the pillows. "There's nothing about her. Just a friend."

"Did you sleep with her?"

"Yes. Years ago." He laughed.

After taking my shower, I returned to the bedroom where Lockie was watching something on television and got into bed next to him.

"Did you love her?" I asked.

He clicked the remote and the screen went black, then he turned off the light. "No."

"Why, then?"

"Do I seem above that to you?"

"Yes."

5

Laughing, he put his arm around me and squeezed tight. "I don't think I deserve such high regard, but I would like to believe it's possible to live up to it in the future."

I felt like crying again. "Did she love you? Does she now?"

"Kitty would settle for me. I would feel fortunate, perhaps, because it would be a comfortable situation, but I wouldn't feel lucky the way I do with you." Lockie kissed me. "Go to sleep, Silly, and dream of the man you imagine I am."

***

I woke before he did and lay motionless, thinking.

The sun rose into our eastern window.

"Are you up, Tal?" he asked rolling over.

"Yes.

"No," he replied.

"No, what?"

"Say it. Whatever it is. I can hear it in your voice."

"You must have hated coming here."

He pushed back the covers and got up.

"Do you think I wrote the journal for you?"

"No."

"Do you think what I wrote was the truth?"

I paused.

"Talia."

"Yes, as you experienced it."

He stood. "Take the morning off and read the rest. I never said I hated it here. I was grateful. Not only was it the only position I could get, the farm is beautiful. It was a blessing for me, a chance to heal. I thought whatever the deal is with these two girls, I'll find a way to improve the situation. I only had a few months, then I'd be unemployed again."

"No one told me that."

"I was hired to get you to the National. It was a time-limited job. What did you think?"

"That you were the new trainer."

"Then what?"

"You'd stay."

"And after you aged out, then what?"

"By the time you settled in, I didn't think about you leaving. Ever."

"Why would you think that if you thought I hated it here?"

"You should have been in shock for the first week! We were horrible to you!"

"Talia, stop it." He pulled a shirt over his head. "This may come as a disappointment, but the two of you are not the most temperamental riders I've ever had to train."

He went down the stairs. "Should I wait for you?"

"You go on ahead."

I heard the front door open and close.

It wasn't a disappointment.

2

HIS TRUCK WAS GONE when I got to the barn. "Where's Lockie?" I asked Cap as she brought Keynote in from the field.

"Acadiana. He went to help Cam."

"Okay. Are we ready for the Zuckerlumpens?"

"I didn't bring the ponies in yet but Beau rolled in a mud puddle."

"That's good," I replied.

Cap regarded me with surprise.

"We'll give them an intensive on how to wash a pony and get it dry before it rolls again."

"What about Miss Ami if she shows up?"

"We'll give her a sponge, too."

"She's not the type to get wet and dirty."

That was true. Ami much preferred clean perfection to looking as though she had exerted herself. Her blingy earrings had to match the color of her shirt. The nail polish was usually a shocking color not found in nature. She always wore a belt.

I counted myself fortunate when I could find my belt. Most commonly, it was used to keep my duffel bag from spilling its contents through my truck.

"Buck should ride in with the girls."

"Cam left a message saying Buck should ride Obilot."

"I thought Cam was riding him in the hunter derby at Rhinebeck next weekend."

"As far as I know, he is."

It seemed a bit odd that so close to a big show, Cam wouldn't be riding Obi himself, but he knew much more about how these strategies were played better than I did. Obi was a good hunter and Cam was a top rider. Maybe there wasn't any training to be done, at the moment, just riding to maintain fitness.

I always had to consider which horse to put in with the girls so the ponies weren't frightened by the traffic. Especially now with Ami who seemed to have a particularly difficult time orienting herself to her surroundings. It was almost as if she had ear buds in and her full concentration was not on riding.

At a horse show, riders were likely to be in a class with horses of all sizes and dispositions. It was good to learn how to deal with a crowd.

"There are no classes at events," Buck protested when he learned he was to ride in with the ponies again and would have to avoid them. "This is something I will never use in the real world!"

I looked at him evenly. "You have five minutes to think about it, and apologize to me or you're not riding. Explain it to Lockie when he gets back."

Buck strode away down the aisle.

In some ways, he had reverted to his old self since he had been living with his father. Buck needed full-time observation and attention. Pete Bouley was constantly trying to conduct business. If he wasn't doing that, he was socializing as a way to conduct business. This was the perfect area for him to take up residence as there were many city people arriving each weekend to pretend to be gentleman farmers and landed gentry. He fit right in.

Unfortunately, Buck didn't fit into this scheme at all and had been much better off with Cam riding herd on him all day with Kate and Kerwin keeping an eye on him during the other non-sleeping hours.

If Pete Bouley had a lick of sense, he would have gracefully bowed out and given Buck the option of where and how he wanted to live. That was the least likely outcome since Pete had proven himself to have the disposition of his own mother, with a reaction to nearly everything of acquiring it for his own.

I hoped Buck would be able to avoid a far too predictable future of being a wealthy playboy, using people and horses as if they were Kleenex. If he returned to the world of the Bouleys that's exactly what I expected his life trajectory would be.

How much of a responsibility did we have to him, especially now that he was living with his father? Legally, none. Morally? I wanted to help Buck but it wasn't an easy path to navigate.

Ami was another issue. As we helped Gincy wash Beau, Ami stayed to the side, feigning interest in Kyff, then Henry, then Obi. She was separating herself from the group and, while I wanted to help Kate Cooper, I had the feeling Ami was not going to become one of us by her choice, not ours.

Cap pushed a comb into her hand and told her to use it on the mane and tail.

"This isn't my pony," she replied.

Anyone who loved horses would be enthusiastic about helping. That one remark told me everything I wanted to know about Ami. She didn't want to be at the farm, learn to ride or work with the ponies.

What were we supposed to do with her for the next two months?

I told the girls to tack up the ponies for the lesson and, with Cap, went to Greer's office.

"What am I supposed to do with Ami Gish when she's expressing less than no interest in riding or the ponies?"

Greer looked up from the screen of her laptop. "Two choices. Send her home now or babysit her until school starts."

"You can't be serious."

"Why can't I be?"

"There is no one on the property who isn't serious about riding. Except her."

Greer shook her head. "Are you forgetting Nicole?"

That was true. Nicole Boisvert was serious about winning, not riding. "She's gone."

The phone rang and Greer picked it up so Cap and I walked out.

"While Nicole was here, we decided to tolerate her. Tolerate this one. Maybe she'll come around," Cap said.

I smiled. "Are you always so practical?"

She shrugged. "Maybe it's just realistic. It's easier if you just set about working with the situation you have than to try to make it conform to what you think it should be."

I was about to agree when I thought better of it. "Wait. No."

"You're doing it." Cap laughed.

"We're here to make things right."

She reached for a pony bridle. "By your definition."

"I'm not an egomaniac," I protested.

"Are you sure?"

Cap was teasing me, I was sure of that. "Yes."

"You can't fix everything. Choose your battles wisely," she replied and went to help tack up Fudge.

Even if our worst moments, I never felt the riding ring was a battlefield, why was it now?

We got the three girls mounted, and since Buck hadn't apologized, he would be cleaning tack under Cap's watchful eye. I had put Gincy on Call because he knew more dressage than she did and that's what we were working on for that lesson. Fudge would pack Ami around the ring. Or so I thought.

The problem was that he expected a certain level of ability and she didn't have it. Ami's knees were nowhere near the saddle flap, which meant her lower leg was turned in, pressing onto Fudge's sides. He thought that meant go, so he went. She didn't want to go so was pulling on his mouth to slow down. Even good-natured Fudge was waving his tail back and forth in displeasure.

I didn't blame him, and brought Ami into the center of the ring where I pressed her knee into the correct position. "Firm contact but don't pinch."

"This isn't how we do it at school."

"Could you try to adopt our style while you're here?" I asked politely.

"What would be the reason?"

"You'll be a better rider."

"But you're doing it wrong. How is that going to make me a better rider?"

My first reaction was to point out that, unlike Ami, I had ridden on the A show circuit and had control of my lower legs, seat and hands, all of which she didn't.

"Okay. You don't need to have lessons here. Your father has arranged for you to ride, so just ride. In September you'll go back to school without any inappropriate teaching."

Ami regarded me blankly. "I still want to show."

"Why? If you're not taking lessons, you're not learning anything and not improving."

"You don't seem to understand," she said raising her voice.

How I wished that Greer were standing next to me. "What don't I get?"

"Am I supposed to go back to school with no ribbons?"

"I have a box full of them in the hayloft. You can have all you want," I replied and went to the center of the ring. "Let's have a nice working trot."

"What am I supposed to do?" Ami asked.

"Ride around. There's plenty of room. Please don't pull on his mouth, you're making him uncomfortable."

"What about me?"

"If you're uncomfortable, you have the choice to get off. Fudge doesn't have the choice to leave you here and go back

14

to his stall. The least you can do is to be considerate of him."

Ami looked at me as though I was a very stupid person.

I knew at that moment that I couldn't teach her anything and there wasn't a pony in the barn, or the state, I would want her to ride.

"Ami, please come to the center of the ring and dismount."

"Why?"

"You're done for the day. And don't take out your irritation with me on Fudge."

She came to the center and slid off. "What do you want me to do with him?"

"Go to the barn and ask Buck to come get him, then ask Cap to drive you home."

"I'm supposed to be here all day," Ami protested.

"Your schedule just changed," I replied. "I think you'll be much happier with Robert Easton for your trainer."

Out of the corner of my eye, I could see Poppy and Gincy with looks of horror on their faces.

"Does he produce winning riders?"

"You'll show every weekend. I'll call your father and explain that I can't provide the kind of experience you're looking for."

"He's in the city," Ami said.

"I'll leave a text message. I hope to see your name and photo in The Chronicle," I called to her as she left the arena.

There was soft applause from the Zuckerlumpens.

"She was mean," Gincy said.

"Ami doesn't know any better," I replied, fully aware that she would not learn anything else with Robert Easton but she'd probably be much happier. And, if she wasn't, I wouldn't have to look at her sour face again and my ponies wouldn't have to tolerate being kicked and pulled all over the farm.

"Would you do that to us?" Poppy asked seriously. "Banish us?"

"I'd spank you first. Take the rail and let's get some work done."

3

JUST BEFORE LUNCH, Lockie stopped me on the way to the house.

"I'd like to speak to you."

"Sure, but I'm not sorry I sent her packing."

Lockie seemed confused as he began to walk beside me. "Who?"

"Ami Gish."

"Excuse me?"

"Isn't that what this conversation is about? You telling me that I should keep the students we have?"

"I was at Acadiana. I have no idea what went on here."

"Now that you know, isn't that what you're going to say?"

"Our business is training horses. If we train some riders along the way, that's fine. Why did you get rid of Ami?"

"She was pulling on Fudge's mouth while banging his sides with her floppy legs."

"And?"

"She was rude to me."

Lockie nodded. "You didn't want to work with her to change that?"

"No, I didn't."

He paused. "What if I had come here and said that?"

"Didn't I say I expected that the first day? I said you would never last. And then we had the protracted discussion about it this morning."

"Talia. Don't make this so difficult. I thought about what you said and it's partially true."

"See."

"You're so quick on the trigger. Think about it from my perspective. I went from upper level competition to training two riders with horses who could not get them to where I was supposed to get them."

I stared at him.

"Sans Egal is a good regional horse but he's not a national level equitation horse. Butch is as honest as horses come but he's not what judges are looking for."

"Why didn't you say that?"

"Your father and I discussed it. When Butch was out of the picture, it was the perfect opportunity to get you on something that would give you a shot. Even though it was in the middle of summer, I found two candidates in Virginia. You wanted CB. Then Greer wound up with a jumper prospect. Those were not my decisions to make. Obviously, neither of you really wanted to get to the National."

I paused on the driveway. "On different horses, could we have made it to Kentucky?"

"I would have made you make it."

"Because you cared about us or because it would have reestablished you in the business?"

"Do you mean that?" Lockie asked in surprise.

"Yes."

"This may come as a disappointment to you, but you sisters were not the be-all end-all in my universe no matter what I had been through. When I have a job to do, I do it one hundred percent. I don't think about parlaying one thing into something else. I don't use people and I don't use horses."

"I know that."

"Why did you say it?"

I thought for a moment.

"Talia."

"I want us to be enough for you and I'm not sure we are."

Lockie put his arm around my shoulders and dragged me to him. He kissed the side of my face hard. "You're too much."

"How do I know?"

"Think back to the winter circuit. I was offered other positions at stables where I would have been riding horses that cost high six figures but I came home. That's how you know."

I sighed.

"What?"

"Tch."

"Say it."

"I wish it was raining," I said.

"It rained two nights ago, it's not dry."

"We could..." I took his hand.

"We'd still ride."

"Then I wish it was eight hours from now."

He squeezed my hand. "We'll go home after lunch for a half hour. Okay?"

"This is how your life is different now."

"Yes, it is," Lockie replied as we continued up to the house. "I never worked at a farm where there was a beautiful girl who wanted to snuggle with me and put flowers in my hair."

"You remember that? It was stupid, wasn't it?"

"It was a gesture made by a person who thinks of herself only after considering the needs of those around her."

"I'm not that considerate," I said. "I want you to have the life you want but I want you to want us. See? Selfish."

"Good point. Would you do anything to keep me here if I wanted to leave?"

"Of course not."

"See? Not selfish."

I shook my head as Lockie held open the kitchen door and walked inside.

"Perfect timing," Jules said. "Bel Miller just arrived with samples from the dessert menu. It's completely unnecessary but delicious."

A curvaceous young woman with dark hair was standing by the counter. Nearby was a selection of pastries the likes I had never seen before. There were shapes, designs, and decorations I wouldn't have imagined possible,

"Hi," Bel said. "This is the last time you'll be able to change your minds."

"Little chance of that," Lockie said as he reached for a glossy chocolate pyramid.

"Don't you want lunch first?" Jules asked, trying not to grin.

"No." Lockie took a large bite of the pastry then nodded his appreciation.

I knew, of course, that there was such a crowd expected that Jules couldn't do all the food preparation herself. A barbecue chef was going to do various smoked meats, and Unspeakably Desirable had been hired to do the fancy pastries. Jules had been making gelato for days so frozen desserts were her contribution. Bread and rolls were coming from an artisanal bakery and rare, white strawberries were being delivered from a nearby farm.

"Don't just consume them," Bel said as Lockie chose one of everything for our plate. "You need to tell me what you think."

"They're great," he replied.

"You haven't tried them all yet," Jules pointed out.

"I don't need to."

I took a small round tart topped with little raspberries. "I'll report back."

"Thank you," Bel replied with a smile.

We brought sandwiches, salad and more pastries back to the carriage house and sat on the terrace for ten whole minutes in peace until the phone rang. A trainer in Maryland was interested in a horse Lockie had gotten a few weeks ago. After that call, there were two others.

"Please turn off the phone during lunch."

Lockie put it on the table in front of us. "What's wrong?"

"One thing is Buck. Have a talk with him. He also was rude to me this morning because he thought he was above riding in with the ponies. So I said apologize or clean tack and he chose to clean tack."

"Why am I the designated enforcer and not you?"

"Because obviously you are a guy and so is he. I don't want to expect him to behave like the girls but these explosive moments are unneeded. You'll approach it from a different perspective than I would."

"Guy to guy."

"Yes."

"I'll talk to Cam first. Is that all right?"

"That's fine. I know Buck has control issues and living with his father has set him back but..."

Lockie nodded. "I understand. Cam and I will come up with something." He paused. "We need a hammock."

"I'll send for one. It'll be here in two days."

"Don't they have any in town?" Lockie asked, standing.

"I don't know, do I? I don't have time to go shopping."

He pulled me to my feet. "Is this what our lives have become? We don't even have time to drive to Greater Metropolitan Newbury?"

"Yes, that would be a correct assessment." I followed him into the house and sat next to him on the saddle tan leather sofa.

"Closer."

I moved the quarter inch nearer and felt his bones. "You're thin."

"I'm not."

I looked at him.

"I'm...wiry."

"You're doing too much and not eating enough. Is that why you ate nearly every pastry we brought home?"

"No, they were delicious."

"Have you been throwing up?"

"All I wanted was five minutes sitting next to you and now it's as though I entered a doctor's office."

"Have you seen Dr. Jarosz for your regular appointment?"

He didn't answer.

"Lockie."

"It's an all day event. I don't have that much time to spare in the summer."

"This is more important than going to town and looking for a hammock. I took the phone out of my pocket. "I'm calling."

"Don't run my life."

I handed him the phone. "Make the appointment."

As it rang, he clicked it off.

"Okay. Next time you're puking your guts out, drive yourself to the hospital."

"You don't mean that," he said.

"Of course not."

We were silent for a minute.

"We were supposed to have Mondays off," I said. "That lasted about three weeks."

"Do you want Monday off?"

"Yes. To take you to the doctor. Or go to the Sound and smell the salt water."

Lockie thought. "Maybe next month."

"Why in August?"

"There's a lot on the schedule this month."

July seemed to be a normal month as far as I knew. There was a show for the Zuckerlumpens, a One-Day for Buck and this Independence Day celebration that was taking longer to organize than it would last.

I was about to ask what he was referring to when we both heard a horse trailer start down the driveway and Lockie glanced out the window.

"Mr. Auerbach and his Belgians."

I stood. "Rufus and Daisy. I have stalls for them in the lower barn."

"You take care of getting them settled and I'll talk to Buck."

"Do you know what you're going to say?" I asked as we left the house.

"I'll try to find out what's going on with him."

"He was better over at the Coopers."

"Kate had practice. She raised Cam, didn't she?"

I nodded. Cam had turned out pretty well.

$\backsim$ 4 $\backsim$

CB NICKERED TO ME as I reached his stall and opened the door to give him a carrot. He stuck his nose out begging.

"You're so spoiled." I handed a piece of carrot over then put my arms around his neck. "Do you want to go cubbing?"

"You're taking my dressage horse cub hunting?" Lockie asked coming up behind me.

"Day thought it would be fun and at least you finish riding before the heat. Come with us. Ride Wing or Henry."

Lockie reached into my back pocket for a piece of carrot. "You do know that taking these upper level horses into the hunt field is not done."

CB took the carrot from him, then turned back to me.

"Why is that? It's bad for them to have a normal life?"

"You know it's a risk. And potentially confusing."

I stroked CB's forehead. "You think he can't hold two thoughts in there at the same time? You imagine he can't avoid stepping on puppies one morning and then do a dressage test another?"

Lockie paused.

"You do think that! How is that different than a three-day?"

"Because on the cross country phase there are no hounds and no other horses galloping next to him."

I shook my head. "I'm not getting it."

"CB has his quirks but he's not a hot horse. Some of the upper level horses are very hot. Over-stimulating them is a poor training choice."

"Is that why people resort to drugs?"

"Yes."

"Maybe if those saddle scorchers were allowed to run free once in a while, they wouldn't have all that pent-up energy," I replied.

"Or maybe they just get confused and think that galloping everywhere is what they're supposed to be doing."

We left CB to his hay and the fan blowing air across him.

"Is that true?"

"From my experience, yes."

"You think that Wing would get the wrong idea about his job?"

"He had a lot of wrong ideas when I got him. Reminding him of his previous life would be counter-productive."

"Ride Henry then."

"Maybe."

"You don't have fun with the horses."

"I can't afford to have fun with them."

"Why is that?" I asked as we went outside.

The glistening flaxen chestnuts, Daisy and Rufus, had been turned out with Butch and the ponies. They were all eating grass with complete contentment. Life, for them, was perfect.

"When they go down the road, one of us shouldn't be crying and that won't be you."

I took his hand. "Do you think that's a good way to be? Setting yourself limitations on how much you'll allow yourself to feel?"

Lockie laughed. "That's a girl question. I separate business from my personal life. Horses are business."

"You didn't feel regret or loss when you left Wing with Dan Ruhlmann?"

"Of course, I did. That was all my life was at that moment, but I didn't cry from Kentucky to Connecticut." Lockie squeezed my hand. "I don't want you to cry."

"That's so sweet," I said, and squeezed his hand in return.

"It's a business decision. We can't afford all the tissues."

"I don't need tissues when I cry in the shower."

Lockie stopped. "Are you hiding your crying from me?"

"Yes."

He sighed. "Good."

Laughing as he opened the kitchen door, I went inside.

***

Cap had a revised schedule for the holiday. Horses still had to be ridden, chores still had to be done even with the tent in the field and guests milling around. After lunch, I was on a sales horse, Lime Street, Cap was on Spare, Day was on Moonie and Greer was on Perfidia, a mare we were keeping for a few months while the owner was out of the country.

"Sit in the saddle not on it," Lockie said, walking to the center of the arena.

"What?" Greer asked.

"Lengthen your legs around the mare's sides and make your lithe self heavy."

"Why am I on this horse?" She asked, narrowly missing the fence. "It's like steering a barge."

29

"Because you're spoiled," he replied.

"I'm done." Greer managed to pull the horse to a halt.

"Will you listen for a moment? You and Tea mindread each other. It's effortless. You're good on Counterpoint. There are other horses with dispositions that are not in sync with yours. You should learn to ride them. Be done now if you want to leave. Outside leg if you want to stay."

Greer got off and handed Lockie the reins. "Show us."

I went into the center of the ring, gave him my helmet and a moment later he was doing a sitting trot on the mare.

"This is what you're doing." Lockie went halfway around the ring. "This is what you should be doing."

Greer looked at me and I shook my head.

"We're not seeing it," I said.

"If you're nervous or annoyed, your muscles tense and you, Greer, are squeezing upward." Lockie demonstrated more clearly. "I'm lighter in the saddle, not as deep. This causes me to lose full use of my legs and seat. No seat, no back."

Cap nodded.

Lockie began trotting a serpentine across the ring. "I understand this mare isn't very responsive and that's because no one ever asked for bending, flexion, or engagement from the hind end."

I sighed.

"He can ride anything," Day commented, watching him go past us.

"You have to be unemotional when you get on a horse." Lockie continued doing the serpentine, getting the horse to bend a little around his leg and not running into the fence with each pass. "You may not like the horse on a personal level, but you need to put that aside and get the job done." Lockie returned to the center of the ring. "I haven't been in love with every horse I've ever had to ride. Some of them were complete strangers, but I had a job to do." He slid off and handed Greer the reins.

"Do you really think Tea and I have a connection?" Greer waited for a leg up.

"Yes, I do. I don't have to lie to you because I already live with your sister and can't get fired."

Cap and I laughed.

Lockie boosted her into the saddle, then handed me my helmet. "Can we get to work?"

We took the rail.

"Sitting trot. You know what's always funny?"

"No, I don't," I replied, steeling myself for the answer.

"When you all think I can't do something I've asked you to do." Lockie laughed.

I decided to ignore him, egomaniac that he was.

"Squeeze the inside rein, Tal."

Did he really need to talk to me?

I squeezed the rein and Lime Street softened in my hands

Apparently so.

We did our twenty minutes, I gave my helmet to Lockie so he could walk Lime down the road with Greer and I returned to the barn to prepare for my pony riders.

There was a young woman walking down the aisle, peering into each stall when I arrived.

"May I help you?" I asked.

"I'm looking for Caprice Rydell. Is she here today?"

"She should be back in a couple minutes. I'm Talia Margolin." I held out my hand.

"That's Emma Crocker," Cap said coming up behind me.

I should have guessed that.

Emma crossed to Cap and gave her a large hug. "I've missed you."

"I missed you, too," Cap admitted. "What are you doing in Connecticut?"

Emma paused. "I'm here to see Mill. And you, of course."

"I don't know where Mill is," Cap replied, continuing down the aisle. "Haven't spoken to him in months."

"He's at Acadiana," Emma called after her.

"Okay. It's nothing to me."

"But we're still friends, right?"

"Of course. You're the first sane person I met in California."

"You have to get used to them."

"I was there almost four years," Cap said.

"That's not long enough. They don't all wear patchouli and surf. I don't do either of those and I was born there."

Cap finished wiping Spare's bridle and hung it up on his rack. "It doesn't matter. I'm not going back. I'm home and I like it."

"Was it so terrible being with us in California?"

"No, I like...liked your family. But it's not my family after all."

The Zuckerlumpens ran down the aisle and Poppy threw herself at me.

"I have to get these girls ready for their ride," Cap said and turned away.

"I'm sorry," I said to Emma. "Mill hurt her feelings."

"I know he did but I thought she could get past it."

"I don't understand. How could she get past it if they haven't spoken in months?"

"I was part of her family, too, and she hasn't spoken to me in months."

"Let's give Cap a little bit of time and maybe she'll feel differently."

Emma nodded, but wasn't convinced. "They were supposed to stay together. How can this make sense?"

"I don't know from experience but I'd say staying together takes a lot of luck and a lot of work. If you don't have one of those elements, people fall away."

"My parents divorced. I really wanted to see it work for my brother," Emma said.

"We want the people we care about to be happy. Do you need anything to eat? Do you need a place to stay?" I asked.

"Mill's taken care of a room for me. It's a big farm."

Following Gincy and Poppy, we walked out to the stable yard together. "Acadiana is a beautiful property."

Lockie and Greer had just returned from their hack.

"This is Emma Crocker," I began.

He slid off Lime Street.

"Hi, Lockie," Emma said.

"Hi, Emma."

"So you've met," I noted.

"When I was over at Acadiana helping Cam."

I nodded. "It was nice to meet you, Emma, I have a training session to do. Feel free to stay as long as you'd like. There's plenty of food at the house."

"Thank you," she said as I began walking away.

What to say to Cap eluded me since even though I was often accused of inserting myself into everyone's business, that was only when I saw another possibility. This was a situation I couldn't begin to grasp. Cap had not been forthcoming with details or her feelings. She said it was over and I took her at her word. This was her decision.

Just as it had been my decision to move into the carriage house to be near Lockie. No one questioned me or tried to talk me out of it. Maybe it just seemed as sensible to them as it did to me. Natural. Predictable.

Maybe that's how Emma felt about Cap and Mill. That they were meant to be together and this separation was a cosmic mistake.

The more I thought about it on the way to the ring, the more I realized I had no opinion. I liked people being happily together. I also liked people just being happy. Cap said she was satisfied with her life as it was now and I accepted it.

This was not a good week for me to problem-solve when in two days we were going to have guests everywhere and asking where the bathrooms were.

Poppy and Gincy were warming up when I stepped into the ring.

"Where's Ami?"

"She not coming back," I replied.

"Told you," Gincy said to Poppy.

"We have a show this month and it's going to be very busy here for the next few days. You're still going to ride but you'll be doing conditioning exercises on the hill."

"Why?"

"There's going to be too much traffic down here for the ponies."

"Okay," Poppy said. "Talia, is it okay if I say something?"

I thought for a moment. Was I going to get a confession to something awful? "Yes."

"We didn't like Ami. She thought she was better than us."

"I'm sorry. Everywhere you go in life you'll find people like that. Ignore them and do the best you can."

"Was she better than us?" Gincy asked walking Beau up to me.

"She knows less about riding and wears more expensive clothes. You decide which is more important to you."

"Being a good rider!" Poppy leaned over and threw her arms around Tango's neck.

That was something Ami would never do. She might get horse dirt on her shirt.

5

WITH FREDDI OUT WITH THE ZUCKERLUMPENS, I went back to the house for ice tea. My grandparents had arrived for the party and Trish Meade was sampling popsicles Jules was making.

I continued on into the house to wash up when my phone rang. "Hi."

"Hi. Where are you?"

"In the kitchen. Where are you?"

"The den," Lockie replied.

I laughed as I went down the hallway and found him sitting at the desk.

"We have a horse coming tomorrow."

"To sell?" I asked.

"To train. It's a mare who has picked up some bad habits this spring and she needs to be convinced out of them for the indoor shows."

"Okay."

"And I got a call from Kitty. She wants to spend a few months here in training."

I didn't say anything.

"You have nothing to be concerned about." Lockie motioned me over to him then patted his leg. "Tal."

Reluctantly, I sat on his lap. "Why you? Is there no one else on the East Coast Kitty can train with?"

He put his arms around me. "She was good to me when I needed help."

I sighed.

"Now she needs a little help. We can do that, can't we?"

What was there to say?

"What are your concerns?"

"People have emotions that are very complicated and sometimes you feel things you didn't intend."

"My feelings aren't that complicated," Lockie replied.

"Maybe hers are."

"No. We're friends. That's it. That's all it ever was."

"I don't feel as though there's a choice."

"Of course there is, you can say no."

"And how will you feel about that?"

"I will be disappointed."

I stood. "Can you understand why I would have reservations?"

"Yes."

"You're really very appealing," I said.

He smiled. "As proven by my reputation on the show circuit."

"Lockie."

"I'm more than two years away from that life. I chose something else."

"Proximity to you may reignite old feelings of hers. I'm not saying yours."

"Reignite?" He reached for my hand.

"I'm trying to find the best words."

"I know you are. Kitty has no passion for me to be reignited. She knows you and I are together."

I nodded. "You can't hold onto someone who wants to leave."

Lockie shook his head.

"Victoria tried to hold on to my father and he just wanted to be with my mother."

"I knew you'd go there."

"That's the template I know," I shot back.

"Learn this new template. Do you really think I'd walk away from you?"

"People I...care about have left me."

"That's true. Can we make a deal?" Lockie asked.

"I don't want to make deals. This isn't about deals."

"Sure it is. Here's the deal. You walk away from me. Okay?"

"I don't know what that means."

"When you've had enough of me, you leave."

"I still don't get it. What if you have enough of me?"

"No, that's not the deal," he said then paused. "I do understand what you're unwilling to say."

I couldn't speak.

"Don't cry. It's a holiday weekend and your family is here."

"Lockie—"

"The only way I'm leaving you is feet first."

"That's a horrible thing to say!"

He laughed and crushed me against his chest.

***

Greer and I went to town and picked up an enormous order of Chinese food then we all sat on the terrace and ate it while watching the sun set on the tent so out of place in our pasture. The horses had gotten used to it but I hadn't.

"It'll be fun," Greer had said to me twenty times since the workers had arrived.

Yes. It probably would be but the pasture was being ruined. It was not that we didn't have other pastures, but this was the one I saw every time I went up and down the driveway. The grass would grow back although it would probably not fill in until fall. These bare spots would be like

40

a scar, a disfigurement on the once perfectly green landscape.

My grandfather told humorous stories and everyone laughed over blueberry pie and lemon gelato. I was certain my grandmother had heard them all before but she laughed along with the rest of us. It wasn't the stories making her laugh, it was how much she loved him coming spilling out.

At the end of the evening, I helped Cap do a final check of the horses and found Lockie waiting for me by the house so we could walk home together. He told me about his plans for training the horses around all the other activities going on and was concerned about the fireworks display on the Newbury Fairgrounds frightening the horses.

It was like thunder and the horses had never been bothered before but that meant the ponies, Butch and Sans Egal. We had no need for hot horses then and now I doubted CB would be bothered by loud noises. A couple beers and he would mellow right out.

Lockie had the fan on in the bedroom when I got out of the shower and crawled into bed beside him.

"I don't want you upset, Tal, but I must say that I'm deriving some enjoyment from seeing that you would miss me if I left."

"How many times have I told you that?"

"I forget," he replied and snuggled his face against my neck.

***

Coming onto noon, a matching dark blue truck and trailer drove into the yard. The only identifying mark was the name Kitty Powell painted in script by the tack room door, barely able to be discerned from a distance.

Greer and I stepped out of the barn as the rig stopped and a blonde woman got out of the truck.

Cam appeared from the upper barn. "Kitty!"

"Cameron!"

She jogged to him, he put his arms around her and, laughing, spun in a circle.

"I haven't seen you since Harrisburg, a year ago, two years ago?" Cam returned her to the ground.

"I quit."

"Why?"

"I needed new challenges. I've been hitting the same shows since I was six. Boring." Kitty turned. "Are you going to introduce me, or should I announce myself?"

"Greer, Talia, this is Kitty Powell. She has a horse in the trailer who wants to get out. Kitty, this is Greer Swope and her sister, Talia Margolin, who would never be accused of being boring."

Kitty stepped forward with a warm smile to shake our hands. "Thank you so much for making it possible for me to come up here and work with Lockie."

"I know he's looking forward to it," I replied. "Cam, you can put her horse next to Henry. We need to get up to the house, but come up for lunch when you're settled in."

Greer began striding away and I had to hurry to catch up to her.

"Don't read anything into it," I said.

"Why doesn't he spin me around?"

"Do you even let him touch you? Do you hold hands?"

"Of course not."

"How is he going to twirl you? That would require human contact."

"If he liked me enough—"

"He does. Remember what happened last time he made an overture to you?"

"You mean Florida?"

"Yes. You overreacted, shall we say."

"We shan't and that was a proposition."

"And, Lady Greer, you could have simply said 'Thank you for your very kind offer, but, at this time, I must decline.'"

Greer looked at me. "You did that better than I do."

"No, I did it exactly like you do since that's where I learned how."

"He'll never ask again."

I shook my head. "Give him an opening and he'll prove you wrong." We reached the terrace where Jules was starting to organize lunch for everyone. "No one knows what you're thinking."

"Me, neither," she replied.

6

FORTUNATELY, chairs had been delivered to the tent so Cam and Lockie liberated enough for everyone wanting lunch.

I don't know how Jules always prepared just the right amount, and couldn't remember a time when someone was disappointed at a meal. Perhaps that came from her years of experience working in restaurants. Jules did have a knack for serving people and we were all glad she chose to do that at the farm instead of her former boyfriend's eatery, Petals or Stems or Tendrils, whatever he called it. Our dinner there, we all agreed, was very close to the worst meal of our lives.

Kitty answered questions about her farm and family, which my father and grandfather were familiar with since it was prominent in the business world. I wasn't aware of any famous Powell company who manufactured anything I would use but that wasn't surprising.

She was at ease with strangers which was a beneficial social skill to possess, and knew when to stop talking about herself and elicit information from others. Cam told a humorous story about a show they had ridden in years ago when the buckles had broken off the girth in the middle of a jumping class.

Through her laughter, Kitty tried to describe how Cam had stayed on, pushed the saddle off, and finished the round bareback. We all laughed, as it was so believable. Cam was part cowboy and all stick-to-itiveness.

Greer did not laugh, and I was afraid she would start crying or worse if I didn't get her away from the table soon.

I pushed my chair back. "Isn't it time to take Joly for a walk?"

He was so useful as an all-purpose excuse.

She looked up at me then stood. "Yes. We'll see you all later." With a slap of her hand against her leg, we were off toward the pond.

When we reached the bench near the water, we sat and let Joly investigate.

"She seems nice," I said after a while.

"She's Lockie's ex-girlfriend."

"She's his ex-something. Current friend now."

"Are you okay with this?"

I sighed.

"Cam probably...she's an ex-something of his too."

"You shouldn't—"

"You're right, I'm sorry. I was extrapolating based on his reputation."

"Greer. You shouldn't say things like that about him either."

"You could say it about me."

"I wouldn't."

"No, you wouldn't."

"Only the present matters. None of us lived flawless lives. Today is..." I thought. "Some people naturally seem to get it right. They're charmed. But, take you, for instance."

"I was hexed by the crone in Little Swerden."

"What?"

"My mother's terriers dug up her flower bed and she put a curse on us."

I laughed. "In the past year you went from being—"

"A bitch, you can say it."

"—to being the best sister a girl could have. That should count for more points because it took work."

Greer watched Joly as he found a frog, touched it with his nose and it plopped into the water to get away from him.

"Some people have a natural affinity for relationships and some of us are just too screwed up."

"No, Greer, it's something we learn," I corrected.

"You and Lockie...do you ever fight?"

"Fight, no. Disagree, yes."

Greer stood and looked out over the pond and fields for a long moment. "I'm going to end up like my mother."

I got to my feet and put my arms around her.

Greer stepped back without looking at me, and slapped her leg. Joly ran to her.

"Your mother is a beautiful woman, enjoying a full life and personal success. She has an amazing daughter and a very eccentric father."

Greer smiled. "That last part is true."

"Be more like your mother."

"No."

"Take risks. Be willing to do something you've never done before. Be uncomfortable. Go up to Cam and take his hand."

She stopped on the path to the house. "What if he..." Greer waved her limp hand in the air.

"Perfect."

"Far from it," Greer replied.

"Then you'll know this is going nowhere. I think that's very unlikely to happen, but why don't you try it and find out?"

Greer shrugged.

We reached the terrace and Jules whirled to face us.

"Next time I see her, I'm going to kill her!"

"Who?" Greer asked

There could only be one answer.

"Fifi!" Jules marched into the house.

We followed.

"What's she done now?"

"She and Robin of Loxley took a runner and went to Italy!"

"Who?" I asked.

Victoria was arranging sandwiches on a platter. "The movie being shot at Rowe House. Fifi fell in love with an actor playing one of the king's knights, and since it was raining non-stop in Little Swerden, Firenza seemed like such a better place to act on their hormones."

"She's under contract," Greer said.

"Trying to follow along," Jules replied in disgust, "is only going to make you dizzy."

"She is very pretty," I commented.

The others looked at me.

"It's given her a misconception of her place in the world."

"My parents spoiled her," Jules admitted as she yanked open the refrigerator door. "Anything she ever wanted, it was hers, immediately if not sooner."

Victoria placed some herbs alongside the sandwiches for decoration. "She went from wanting a colorful piece of candy, to wanting colorful man candy."

"Ugh," Greer replied.

"Maybe you can include that in your next book," I suggested.

"Maybe so." Victoria smiled. "It's not a rare character trait."

"She said, speaking from experience," Greer said.

"I do appreciate an attractive man," Victoria admitted. "That's what makes the world go around. I wasn't attracted to some hobo on the street. I was attracted to your father. If I hadn't been, no you."

"His financial stability didn't hurt."

"Of course it didn't. We haven't evolved that far from the Neanderthals. A man who is a good provider gets the pick of the crop."

I laughed as Greer shot me a warning look. "She's yanking your lead shank."

"Darling," Victoria said, passing Greer on the way to the terrace and giving her a pat on the hand, "you marry a hobo if you like. I'm sure you'll be very happy wearing someone else's clothes dug out of the dumpster behind the Goodwill store."

"Coming from someone who thinks the Chanel boutique on *La Croisette* is equivalent to the corner market," Greer retorted.

Jules laughed. "That's Fifi's favorite hangout."

"She has good taste, if little else," Victoria called from outside.

Sometimes I understood why Jules didn't go home very often.

7

MY FATHER CAME HOME mid-afternoon and had iced tea on the terrace with the men who had come to talk to him.

When I returned to the barn to help the Zuckerlumpens, I had a sense of foreboding that I couldn't put words to.

We worked for twenty minutes, then Freddi took them out for a walk. There would be no more lessons for them until the holiday was over no matter how hard they protested but they and their families would be at the party.

"Where's Buck," Lockie asked, walking up to me.

I let CB's hoof return to the aisle floor. "Home with his father. He did his chores and rode this morning, then Pete brought him home so they could spend the holiday with the grandmother."

"He should have been left with the Coopers," Lockie commented, heading to the tack room.

"Why?" I called after him.

"They managed to do a pretty good job with Cam, right?"

I doubted if Cam had ever been as difficult as Buck. Cam was high-energy, bright and confident. Buck didn't have two loving parents or anything that could be considered a stable home life. He could barely read when he arrived at Bittersweet, and was impulsive and not in a good way. After working with him for the past months, Buck seemed to be settling in and then he overstepped the bounds with me. I could tolerate quite a lot but a lack of courtesy was not on the list.

Lockie appeared from the tack room. "Let's call it a day."

I looked at him carefully. His eyes seemed okay, but he seemed to be tired. "Do you have a headache?"

"Not yet. I'm avoiding one. It's hot. We've been working since dawn. Everyone's had enough."

"I'll have to come back later and put CB out."

"Fine."

He unclipped the crossties and returned CB to his stall, then we left the barn.

"Is there anything to eat at the house?"

"You don't feel well."

"Let's not push our luck. Tomorrow is going to be loud and hot."

We got in the truck and headed up the driveway. "You don't have to stay at the party the entire time."

"I can't be a no-show."

"Yes, you could be," I replied.

"There's business to be done. I'm the trainer at the farm. People want to see me. Some things you just need to do whether you want to or not."

He parked in front of the house.

"If you have a choice," I started, "whipping yourself to do things you don't want to do seems like a punishment you wouldn't inflict on anyone else."

Walking up the steps, he paused at the door. "I'm not whipping myself to attend the party. Sometimes," he went inside, "you accept temporary discomfort."

Opening the refrigerator, I tried to find food for dinner. "I'll keep my eye on you."

"Of course you will."

He went to the desk and began making notes on the day's training sessions.

There were several chicken cutlets in the freezer that Jules had sent down so I put them in the oven with potatoes dauphin and began making a salad.

"Tali," he called from the living room. "Greer's here."

I heard footsteps then the door opened.

"He went out with Kitty," Greer said.

She ate with us, had blueberry sorbet for dessert, then finally left not feeling any better, even though Lockie explained that Cam and Kitty were old friends from the show circuit. Unconvinced, Greer left for home.

The day was finally over.

***

"Do you think my father will make an announcement today," I asked as we drove up to the barn through the thin light of morning.

"I have no idea," Lockie replied.

"None?"

"Your father wouldn't confide something like that to me." He parked the truck in our usual space.

The air was still damp from the night but that would burn off in a couple hours.

"Sure he would. If he's going forward with this run for political office, arrangements must be made."

"With me?"

We walked into the barn where Cap was already starting to bring horses in from the field.

"My father relies on you. You manage the farm."

"I don't see how that is significant to him. I'll still be here."

I went to get the feed cart. "We just started being a real family."

"And?"

55

"What if he moves to Washington?"

"He'll commute," Lockie replied.

"It won't be the same."

"Why don't we work it out when and if it happens?"

"I like to be prepared," I replied.

"You will never be prepared for every eventuality no matter how hard to you try."

The horses heard the cart, and knowing it meant breakfast, began to nicker.

Lockie came to help me. "It wouldn't be forever, just a couple years."

I glanced toward him.

"Okay. That's not a good argument for you but it's the truth. You managed while I was in Florida for most of the winter."

That was true. It was difficult but it was only a few months and Lockie was able to return home frequently. If my father lived in Washington, there would be demands on his time. It would be more like the past, when he was so involved in the business that we rarely ate dinner together. I barely saw him. I barely knew him. That wasn't the life I wanted for us.

"Everything will change," I said.

"Nothing important," Lockie replied.

Cap came down the aisle leading Wing and CB. "There's a trailer coming down the drive. Anyone know anything about it?"

"No," Lockie replied as he went to the door.

Cap looked at me and I shook my head as I followed Lockie outside.

"Long time no see!" A tall man called loudly as he stopped the truck and got out.

"Dan?"

"That's my name."

A woman got out of the passenger side and came over to us. "Lockie." She put her arms around him.

"What are you doing here?" He asked.

Dan and Wynne shared a look.

"This would be a hard secret to keep," Wynne said. "Once we came down the drive, you'd recognize the rig."

"Why is it a secret?" Lockie turned to me. "Tal?"

Wynne smiled. "She called and invited us up for the holiday. She thought you might like to see us. I know you have a terrible temper but don't be mad at her."

The Ruhlmanns laughed.

A horse stamped in the trailer.

"We brought you something to sell." Dan went around to the back of the trailer. "If no one's too busy, can I get some help?"

Lockie left my side and went to get the ramp.

"Thank you for calling," Wynne said to me. "I've missed him so much but I thought if he wanted to see us, he would have made the effort."

"He's so busy," I replied.

"Is he feeling alright?"

"Most of the time. He has good days and less good days."

"Not eventing?"

"No. We managed to talk him out of that. He does everything else. Sometimes it makes me crazy."

Wynne grinned. "Only sometimes? He always made me crazy."

There was the sound of hoofs on the ramp then Dan led a large dark bay horse to the center of the yard. "He's got a good start."

"Why don't you sell him?" Lockie asked.

"Because we just got three prospects in and someone had to leave. There's a limit to how many horses I can bring along," Wynne replied. "Dan's off doing his eventing thing while I'm home doing all the grunt work."

"Trade," Dan said.

"I never cared about competition," Wynne admitted to me.

"Tal doesn't either," Lockie told her.

"Then we have lots in common. We both have nothing to prove and both like Lockie."

"Lockie's not hard to like," I replied.

"Are you serious?" she asked.

"You don't have to enumerate his faults," Dan said. "Let's talk about this horse. His name is Available because he was and he has a huge gallop stride."

"Is he off the track?"

"We got him at a yard sale about six months ago," Dan replied. "He has all the bloodlines you could want, but the owner went bankrupt before any dreams of a Triple Crown win could materialize."

"Nice disposition. Willing," Wynne added, "but he's not for someone who lacks confidence. He's has his own agenda and is committed to it."

"I don't have a buyer for him," Lockie said. "I don't know how fast I can get this done."

"Not a problem."

Living full time in the shed was in Keynote's future, because we were running out of stalls. I hadn't expected Kitty to arrive with her horse, Nearkis, nor Lockie and Cam to bring in two sales horses in June. The upper barn had been full months ago and now with the ponies, there wasn't a spare stall in the lower barn.

I tried to think of someone who could go outside during the day with a fly-sheet on. It wasn't CB, who was very hard on his clothing. He much preferred being naked as proven by the sheet that had been ripped, and repaired, three times until it couldn't be put back together again. He needed chain mail.

Keynote didn't have enough energy to rip his clothing, so he could go out until we could figure out something else. I wondered if anyone could go to Victoria's for a few weeks until some of ours could be rehomed.

"Where do you want him?" Dan asked.

Lockie looked to me.

"Keynote's stall," I replied. "Let Cap take care of it. Would anyone like breakfast?"

"We've been on the road all night, so real food sounds wonderful," Wynne replied.

Lockie and Dan took the horse into the barn while Wynne and I began walking up to the house, passing the beginning of activity at the tent. The barbecue chef had arrived earlier and the scent of apple wood smoke was wafting over the hillside.

"You don't do anything in a small way here, do you?"

"We're combining every summer celebration into the one event. My father has business and political associates who need to be—"

"Entertained?"

"That's a good a word as any. My sister has a charity, so that's another aspect. And...every once in a while Lockie seems to think I'm missing out on life and should go to a square dance."

Wynne laughed.

"So I arranged for a dance floor in the tent and a band, and we'll be square dancing this evening."

She put her hand on my arm. "I'm glad he found you."

I shrugged. "I guess my life prepared me for him."

"Good. Now I can stop worrying."

8

GUESTS BEGAN ARRIVING soon after we finished breakfast. Among the first were men in polo shirts so crisp, they were either never washed before or had been ironed. My father took them into the den and they stayed there.

Trish Meade, Oliver, and the 4-H Club showed up, excited and enthusiastic to get a grand tour of the barn as well as an introduction to all the ponies given by Poppy and Gincy. Watching as Mr. Auerbach harnessed Rufus and Daisy, the girls listened intently as he explained the history and the function of every part of the equipment in detail. Then they were the first to be given a ride on the wagon.

I found Jules overseeing the food service as guests were already lining up for coffee and the homemade blueberry and strawberry filled glazed donuts provided by the women who made the Oliver popcorn balls. After being handed a small bag of still warm donut holes, Jules and I sat at one of the tables.

"So Wynne Ruhlmann is from Connecticut," Jules said.

"Is she? I didn't know."

"Grew up near the Coopers actually."

I sighed. "Have you seen Cam? He left yesterday evening with Kitty and—"

"I know. Greer's upset. This is something she has to work out for herself." Jules finished her coffee. "I have to start organizing the lunch service."

"This is all about food for you today. Are you going to find any time to celebrate and enjoy yourself?"

"Probably after dinner."

"That's hours from now," I pointed out.

Jules nodded. "Don't worry about me. I have plenty of help."

"If you need anything, let me know."

Jules kissed my cheek. "Why don't we have a girls' day out like we used to?"

"That sounds wonderful. Just the two of us?"

I remembered the lunches we had at the Inn, the shopping excursions, trips as simple as going to the farmer's market. There hadn't been much time for those outings in the past few months and I had missed them.

She smiled and nodded.

I was nearly ready to say yes when a thought crossed my mind. "Won't Greer feel left out?"

"Invite her and we'll have a girl to girl to girl chat over shumai." Jules hugged me.

"Konichiwa, the Japanese restaurant. We haven't been there in months."

"The barn manager doesn't give you any time off. I'll have to discuss this imposition on your life and lunch with him," she replied.

"He's so single-minded."

"He needn't be."

"I don't want to interrupt anything," Victoria said as she approached us.

"But you always do," I replied.

"This time I have a good excuse. You have an univited guest making his appearance...now." Victoria pointed to the entrance.

People began hurrying toward the exit, leaving food on the tables, tipping chairs over, sending drinks flying as Partial Stranger strolled in studying everything with great interest.

"That's Greer's colt," I said, then realized I wasn't wearing a belt. "Does anyone have a belt?" I called out but there were so few people left.

"There is a point to leaving halters on when you turn them out," Victoria said.

"It makes me nervous."

Victoria laughed. "And this doesn't?"

"No."

Spotting some greenery decorating a platter, I ran to grab a handful then approached the colt. "What are you doing?"

He stretched out his neck to see what I was offering him and put the lettuce in his mouth.

A moment later, Gincy and Poppy ran into the tent carrying a bucket with grain and a halter and lead rope.

"He got out by himself, I didn't leave the gate open," Gincy said.

I pulled the halter over his head. "No one's blaming you and it's no big deal that he's out. One of you go get a fork, and clean up after him while I take him back to the barn."

We walked out of the tent and headed to the barn as I tried to think of an empty stall to put him in. Since it was the middle of the day as well as the beginning of the festivities, as many horses as possible had been taken out of the pastures.

"How did you get out?" I asked the colt, knowing a walk along the fence-line was in my future. The feeling he was jumping out was becoming more insistent and I didn't doubt it was possible but the fence managed to keep everyone else in.

"I've been looking for you," Lockie said, as he came out of the barn.

He had changed clothes since I saw him last and was wearing civilian clothes—trousers, a plaid cotton shirt, a tie and polished paddock boots.

It made me wonder why someone hadn't started a fan page for him on MyFace.

"What?" he asked.

"What do you mean?"

Lockie brushed off his shirt. "You're staring. Do I have hay on me? Or worse?"

I shook my head. "It was one of those moments where you see something again for the first time."

"Tali, I need to talk to you."

Parti pushed his head against my shoulder.

"Okay."

"Give me the horse. What are you doing with him?"

"He came into the tent looking for Greer or a fresh salad." I handed Lockie the lead rope. "I don't know how he got out and the girls didn't either. They said they didn't leave the gate open."

"He's jumping out," Lockie said.

"He's two years old."

"And?"

"He can't jump that high."

Lockie led the colt down through the barn. "Explain that to him."

"Are you sure?"

Lockie put him in the stall where we had been storing the hay cart, removed the halter, removed the hay cart and shut the door.

"Yes, I'm sure."

"What are we going to do about it?"

"Nothing. You learn to live with these quirks. You live with me so we know you can," Lockie replied and took my hand. "Talia, I want to say something."

"It sounds serious."

"It is."

"Am I going to freak out?"

"No. Tal. This is taking longer than it should. You called Dan and Wynne and invited them up here for me."

"Yes."

"Why?"

"After reading your journal, I understood how important they were to you and thought you might like to see them again. I hope I didn't do the wrong thing."

Lockie dropped my hand and put his arm around my shoulders.

"Silly, that was very thoughtful."

"But?"

"There's no but." He paused. "Small one."

"I knew it."

"You did not know it. I just wish life treated you as well as—"

"No. I don't deserve that compliment. I try to get things right. When I do, it's sheer luck. My mother used to say we're here to do good. I didn't feel what that meant until–"

"I had nothing to do with it. You are just expressing your character."

"Lockie, it's so much more complicated than that."

"No, it's not."

"Was I so wonderful to you when you arrived? Was that my character?"

"Okay, so through me, you saw something in yourself, seeds that your mother had planted began to grow. Remember the good things about her," he said. "Now I have to go see some people about a horse."

We began walking toward the tent.

"You look beautiful today," Lockie said. "You have pretty good legs, too. You should wear a dress more often."

"We should go out so I can."

"Good idea. I have a free day between indoors and Florida."

Because we were in public, I couldn't kiss him.

67

9

AFTER SPENDING MOST OF THE AFTERNOON being sociable, I felt as though I had met nearly everyone in the county. I found Greer watching Trish and Oliver perform to the delight of the crowd that had gathered around them.

"She really is wonderful with Oliver," I said to Mrs. Meade.

"It's easy because they love each other so much."

"Do you think this is what she'll do for a career?"

"Definitely. She's been talking about training service dogs since before getting into 4-H. It's important work, and there are never enough dogs to fill the need."

"Does my sister know?"

"Yes. Greer arranged for Trish to take a two-week course in Ohio next month. She's so excited. But sad, too. Trish doesn't want to leave Oliver."

"I understand. It's such a great opportunity to extend her knowledge, there won't be much time to be homesick."

"Thanks for reminding me. I wanted to ask if it is possible for you to take on the girls in advanced riding program of the 4-H?"

"Hasn't Sue Reif been teaching them for years?"

"Yes, but she has a family situation out of state, and there's no way to predict when she'll be back."

"They're not beginners, assure me of that," I said. "I don't think I'm prepared for that."

"No, they're good riders. I'm not saying they have the financial resources of other kids."

"That's fine. I just want them to be able to stay on."

We didn't have the schoolmaster type horses that were appropriate mounts for absolute beginners. Even Call could be a handful for Poppy. Oh Fudge was less willful but he reacted to whatever aids he was given. If that meant a loose leg improperly applied to his side, he accommodated that request, much to Ami Gish's continued annoyance.

I hoped some of these girls had their own horses and a way to transport them to the farm for lessons. It was good to ride a variety of horses but always best if the student knew how to ride their own horse first.

Everyone applauded Trish and Oliver as they finished their performance, and came over to us.

"Go have a popsicle," I told her. "And I think Jules made a special treat for Oliver, too."

Trish's face lit up. "What is it?"

Jules had made frozen blueberry yogurt into the shape of dog biscuits. Joly had sampled them the previous day, and pronounced them excellent, his tail wagging double-time.

"Go see for yourself," Greer replied.

Mrs. Meade, Trish and Oliver hurried off to the cart where Jules was handing out the gourmet popsicles.

"Did you have a macaron?" I asked.

"I haven't had time."

"Bel made them in an astonishing choice of flavors and colors, at least go look at them."

We made our way through the crowd to the dessert table, where pastries were being restocked continually. I couldn't imagine how many had been delivered to the farm but it had to be hundreds.

"Have you seen Cam?" Greer asked.

"No, I haven't."

"Have you seen Kitty?"

"No."

"Nothing else needs to be said."

"Stop it, Greer." I picked up an intensely pink colored macaron with pastry cream oozing out the side in the most tempting fashion and bit into it. "This is a thing of beauty," I said. "Have one."

Greer picked up one from the line labeled green tea and sampled it. "Good." She shrugged.

"Don't compare it to what Jules does. Bel is also an expert, maybe even more than Jules because she specializes in pastry."

"Heresy!" Greer finished the cookie and stopped. "There's Cam."

I turned and found him at the entrance. "Who's he with?"

"Tal, I think that's Teche."

10

TECHE WAS SO THIN, his weight loss gave it away for me. I knew immediately why we hadn't seen him in months.

"I'm sorry I didn't get here sooner," Lockie said coming up beside me. "I wanted to prepare you."

"You can't prepare people for this."

"A heads-up then," he replied.

"No," Greer said. "I think this explains a lot."

I turned to her. "Like what?"

"Why we have half his horses at our barn. That—"

"You knew," I said to Lockie. "You could have told us."

"He asked for us to keep his secret," Lockie replied. "I couldn't break the confidence. You wouldn't want me to have done that, even for you."

"Is he..."

"Since he's here, he's improving. Teche spent a long time back home in Louisiana. A few weeks ago, he came to Connecticut. He wanted to see Cam ride."

I looked across the tent and it brought back memories.

"Don't go there," Greer said sharply.

"Is more being done for him than what was done for my mother?"

"I said don't go there!"

Lockie took my hand. "Talia, Greer's right. Those aren't the kind of questions you should be asking."

"What are the questions?"

"The same questions you asked about your mother and found the answers for. The same questions you ask about me, Greer, and everyone else you know. What can I do?"

I didn't feel like I could go through it again. Not now, maybe not ever. Even if he wasn't family, even if I didn't know Teche as well as Lockie and Cam did, how could I go up to him and pretend. It had been impossible with my mother. I didn't have the acting gene. I wasn't good at deluding myself. As difficult as the truth was, I preferred that instead of keeping my sunny side up.

Somehow, my mother and father managed to live well those last months. It was beyond my understanding then, but I had come to believe that her illness drew them closer together. Their relationship deepened as the unimportant aspects of daily routine fell away and what was left became concentrated.

Maybe because time was running out and every moment had to count. That was always true, but we just preferred to ignore that reality. It was easier to go about each day as though there was an endless supply of them.

Seeing Teche, made me wish Lockie hadn't gone through his accident alone. He had the Ruhlmanns in Kentucky and they were very good to him, but I couldn't help but think that if I had been there, I would have made the recovery better for him.

Reading his journal had been so painful for me because of all he didn't say was so obvious. I could have sat beside him and reminded him of the word blanket. I wouldn't have let him roll himself out into the rain and stay there for who knows how long.

Yes, I would have hovered. He needed someone there to hover.

He still did.

My mother said that if you care about someone, you care for them. The emotion isn't enough, it must be accompanied by action.

I thought I probably overdid it, but it was better than underdoing it. There shouldn't be a time when Lockie wondered how I felt about him. The same held true for my father, Greer, Jules, and all the horses. No one should ever come to me for help and find I had something more important to do.

But, as I looked at Teche across the tent, my mind was blank. I didn't have one idea what I could do for him.

Spiced blueberry jam filled beignets?

I'd ask Jules who was always quick with suggestions.

Greer was glaring at her mother sitting with Teche. "This is too bad to be true, so it can't be."

"Why not? They've been friends for months."

"Does the word friend ever apply to my mother?"

"Whatever was in her mind last year I suspect is quite different than now. She has a rather perfect life."

"A bestselling book but no man."

"We don't know what she does in her spare time," Lockie remarked.

I nodded. "If Victoria wanted a man, she could have one. She's that kind of woman. It's an innate skill."

Lockie laughed.

Greer did not find this amusing. "Tracy would have mentioned it."

"Victoria and Teche are adults. She's fun. He needs fun."

Greer turned to stare at Lockie. "She's fun?"

"It's the guy perspective," I said.

"Yes, it is," Lockie agreed, taking my hand and leading me to the popsicle stand.

As we reached Jules, the Long Mountain Band took the stage and began to play traditional folk songs starting with one I recognized "The World Upside Down". At the line "If ponies rode men and grass ate the cows" Lockie looked at me in confusion.

"Did I hear that right?"

After giving it a lick, I held out my mango raspberry popsicle, which was a beautiful orange color studded with whole red fruit, for him to taste. "Yes."

"Confusing and delicious, in that order," he replied.

"I have to blow this popsicle stand," Jules announced.

"Why?" I asked in amazement.

She opened the freezer door. "I'm almost out. I didn't count on every guest wanting one or we would have had to start freezing these last month."

"If you need any help, let me know," I replied.

"In about an hour," Jules said, "meet me at the house."

"Okay."

Lockie stepped outside the tent and I followed him.

"Too loud?" I asked.

"Yes. Would it be okay if I disappear for a couple hours?"

"Of course."

"I gave Dan and Wynne the barn tour. They loved CB, but they don't know him."

As it started down the stick, I caught a drip of mango juice with my tongue. "I'm sure you enlightened them."

"Every sin," Lockie replied.

"He's a good horse," I insisted.

"He would not be disappointed if I took up another sport."

"I don't feel that's true. I think he tests you."

"And I'm failing?"

I finished the last of my popsicle and threw the stick into the trashcan. "CB has a sense of humor. He wants to play and you're always so serious with him."

Lockie was about to say something in his defense.

"You're a professional. You have high expectations. Give him some room to breathe. He may never be the dressage horse you want, but CB may be a great partner."

"That's what he reserves for you."

"I think he would like to play with you, too. Give him a chance," I suggested.

"I've never—"

"Start. They're not all the same. They have different personalities and different needs. Different visions of the world."

"They're just horses."

"They're horses but they're not just. They understand more than you think and their feelings are more complicated than running away from an airborne plastic bag."

Lockie thought for a moment and dropped his popsicle stick in the trash. "Do you think Wingspread has the personal depth of CB?"

"If you gave him the room to become himself, probably, yes." I could see Lockie doubted what I was saying. "He's smart, isn't he? He got you around all those difficult courses. He did the dressage tests. Do you think he's intellectually challenged?"

"I never thought about it."

"Why don't you give both of them a chance this summer? You have nothing to lose."

"Be more like you?"

I laughed. "No, but more like the rider you can be. Grow, not only learn. Let them do the same. We owe it to them."

"I'll think about it at home. Come visit if you have the time."

"Bring flowers?"

His smile would have convinced anyone else he was fine.

"Pavel just manicured every blade of grass on the farm, so it won't be clover this time."

"You'll find something. See you later."

I watched him walk away thinking that if he slept until late afternoon, he would probably be able to join us for dinner. If we were lucky, people wouldn't notice his absence.

Turning, I nearly bumped into my father.

"I've been looking for you," he said.

"Anything in particular?"

"Let's take a little walk away from the guests."

We went toward the pond.

"Is everything okay?" I asked.

"That's what I was going to say to you."

"Lockie went home to take a nap. I'm sure you saw Teche."

"Yes. We had a talk and I left him with Victoria overseeing him."

"She wouldn't use this moment in his life to take advantage of him, would she?"

"She would not. I wish you two could know her better."

"I hardly know her, but Greer does and let's put it this way, her mother hasn't made a positive impression on her."

"Victoria is a product of her environment as we all are."

We reached the bench by the water and sat.

He was quiet for a moment. "Time is finite."

"Why are you reminding me?"

"Are you so sure I said it for your benefit?"

I thought. "No. Have you made a decision?"

My father shook his head, then patted my leg. "Your mother would be very proud of you."

"Maybe," I said. "Let me ask you this. If she was still alive, would you be considering running for office?"

"That isn't an easy question to answer."

"Try."

"If she hadn't become ill, I imagine we would have thought it would have been a good idea. If she had survived, nothing would have pried me away."

I nodded.

"Victoria has much to offer. She has many skills but interpersonal relationships are not at the top of the list. I believe she regrets this. Still that's no reason to give up on her."

My father stood and held his hand out to help me to my feet.

I hugged him.

"What would you like me to do?"

"Selfishly, I would have you stay home," I replied. "Time is, after all, finite."

He smiled. "Selfishly, I would."

We began to walk back to the tent and I knew how difficult this decision was for him. If running for public office were for self-aggrandizement, it would have required no reflection at all. The ego doesn't pause for considerations, it just races toward what it wants.

But service is complicated, and carries no expectation of reward. I didn't envy my father this choice.

My father kissed me as we reached the tent and split up, he to his friends, and me to find Jules to see if she needed my assistance.

I had barely taken two steps when Poppy ran up to me, followed by Gincy.

"That new horse attacked her," Poppy said.

❧ 11 ❧

EYES FILLED WITH TEARS, Gincy held out her bleeding arm.

"Which horse," I asked, grabbing a napkin off a nearby table, and wrapping Gincy's arm in it.

"Icky," Gincy said.

I thought she was more shocked than hurt, but something had happened. "Nearkis?"

Gincy nodded. "I didn't do anything to it."

"We were just walking by," Poppy explained.

Greer approached. "What's going on?"

"Kitty's horse bit Gincy," I replied, hoping there would be no discussion.

"I'll take her to the nurse," Greer said and led Gincy away.

"You were walking past the stall and the horse went after you?"

"Yes."

"You didn't try to pet her nose and you weren't dancing and singing or doing something that might frighten her?"

By now, all our horses were used to music, glitter, laughter and strange treats, but Kitty's horse probably lived a very sheltered life without little girls bouncing down the aisle.

"No. I promise, Talia, we weren't loud or obnoxious."

I gave Poppy a hug. "You may be lots of things but obnoxious isn't one of them. Until we understand what happened, you two stay out of reach of that horse."

"I promise. For both of us."

Kitty came up to us, Cam one step behind. "Cap told me something happened. Is this the girl?"

Poppy shook her head.

"Greer took Gincy to the nurse."

"Nearkis nipped her?"

"Gincy was bleeding, so it was more like bit."

"I can't believe it," Kitty said. "She's such a nice mare. I've never had a problem with her."

"She is in a new barn," Cam pointed out.

"It's not as though she hasn't traveled before," Kitty replied. "Where's the nurse? Does the girl need to go to a hospital? Plastic surgery?"

"I think she'll be fine," I replied.

"I'll show you where she is," Poppy offered and off they went.

"I'm sorry," Cam said after a moment.

"It wasn't your fault and these things happen. Horses are unpredictable.

"How is Greer taking it?"

"The accident or Kitty's arrival?" I asked him.

Cam raised an eyebrow.

"Have you ever been to an amusement park, and you go into the Fun House. There are the wavy mirrors, the maze or corridors, puffs of air shooting at you."

He nodded.

"I went into one with some friends from school. The misfit kids. The floor moved back and forth and up and down. With each step, it was impossible to know how your foot would land. It's hard to walk and keep your balance. I think that's how life had been for Greer for quite a long time."

"It doesn't have to be," Cam said.

"It does. That's how she works through things."

"How long does it take?"

"Do you have somewhere else to be?"

He shook his head.

***

I helped Jules in the kitchen, as the shift began from nibbles and noshes to dinner. There was something for everyone and I was happy about that having been to parties where I had been relegated to eating the fruit decorating the middle of the table.

My grandmother helped us until my grandfather insisted she come meet some people. That seemed to be one of the chief benefits of the gathering—people meeting people they never would have otherwise.

Greer would not have liked to hear me say it but Victoria was functioning as an excellent hostess, making sure guests were introduced to each other and knew where to find food and drink. I saw that she had stashed Teche in a corner away from all the excitement and checked on him regularly, bringing him new people to meet or to refill his iced tea glass.

Since Victoria had gotten her own house, she must have spent more time than I realized meeting residents from the area. She seemed to know everyone, and they seemed to be genuinely glad to see her.

When I left the tent, Victoria had just brought Cam's parents, Kate and Fitch Cooper, to see Teche. With nothing left to do, I decided to go home, relax for a while, wake Lockie, and change for dinner.

My father was walking on the driveway, deep in thought, as I reached the edge of the field and fell into step alongside him.

"Whatever you choose is okay with me."

He smiled. "They are trying to persuade me, like a young man trying to assert his virility to his date."

"Got it."

"They will say anything. I am the smartest, most clever, most amusing—"

"And you have the shiniest hair," I added.

He ran his hand through his hair as if to preen. "I do, don't I?"

I nodded.

"So it begins, with flattery. Most people enjoy that so they're hooked quickly."

"But you're immune," I replied.

"I hope I am. Here at the farm, you and Greer keep me humble, but this process is so much about ego."

"Humble? We keep you running for the aspirin!"

"Not true. Well, sometimes it is. What do you think about this opportunity?"

"Me or what do I think Mom's counsel would be?"

"You."

I thought for a moment. "We're a family who tries to serve others. That's how I was raised. That's how you were raised. The question is what is the best way to serve. I'm not even sure for myself. Greer does so much more than I do with her Ambassador of Good Cheer Project."

"You're reading the situation incorrectly, Talia."

"I ride horses. Well but not expertly. I teach horseback riding to a few young girls. Someday soon I will have taught them everything I know and they'll have to move onto a real trainer."

"You're selling yourself short."

"We should be realistic."

"I am very realistic and that's a quality I admire in Lockie. He has a very different opinion of your abilities than you do."

I smiled. "You're both biased."

He put his arm around me and squeezed. "We are but not about this. My grandfather used to tell me that we are always where we're supposed to be. We might not know why and it might not be what we choose but there's something there for us to do. When the task is done, we'll move on."

We were approaching the carriage house. "I don't know."

"I think we always know. Something inside insists louder and louder until it gets our attention. Then we act. It could be a much more streamline process if we would just do that thing immediately." He smiled then leaned over to kiss me.

"But it's not always obvious, is it?"

"No. I'll see you two later." My father said, returning to the company.

86

Going up the walk to the front door, I then entered the house. There was silence. He should have been up by now as it had been a couple hours.

I went into the bedroom and he was still sleeping. It was nearly five and the dinner festivities were starting in about an hour.

I put my hand on his arm. "Lockie. Would you like to get up or keep sleeping?"

He rolled over. "What time is it?"

"Five."

He patted the bed beside him. "Ten minutes."

12

I KICKED OFF MY SHOES and lay down next to him.

"What amazing things did I miss?"

"The Long Mountain Band was good. I helped Jules at the house. Gram was there, too. And Kitty's horse attacked Gincy."

Lockie yawned. "I didn't hear you right. What did the horse do?"

"Poppy and Gincy were walking by and it bit her arm. It was bleeding, not a deep wound, but Greer took her to the nurse."

"I rode it. It's a nice horse."

"Not that nice this afternoon."

"It's a mare," he said.

"What does that mean?"

"I'm not suggesting anything beyond the fact that mares can be a little mareish. She just arrived. There's a huge party, lots of noise and two little girls skipping past."

"Tea's never taken a bite out of one of us."

He held me closer. "So you told Kitty and she defended her horse and blamed the girls."

"No. No, it wasn't like that."

"She's a nice woman. She'll come to be your friend, too, if you let her." Lockie paused. "Kitty needs friends."

"Excuse me?"

"She tries hard but most people can't get past the idea of her family situation." He laughed. "It's like being from the wrong side of the tracks."

"The other wrong side."

"Yeah." Lockie gave me a squeeze and started to get up slowly.

"Did you take your meds?"

"No, I just went to sleep."

"I'll get your pills. Take your shower. Get your hearing protectors and we'll be on our way."

Twenty minutes later, we had reached the barn. I wasn't dressed for it, but there I was in a nice dress and shoes that had never come in contact with manure.

The moment I stepped inside, I knew we should turn around immediately.

"You could have told me," Cap said.

"I couldn't," Mill insisted.

"Of course, you could. It's not as though it was a National Security secret and you could be thrown into jail."

"Teche asked for confidentiality from all of us."

Cap looked to Lockie.

"Do you want us to leave?" I asked.

"I just want to take a look at Kitty's mare," Lockie said. "But I can do that later."

"I live my life in public anyway," Cap said. "I don't have anything to hide. I don't have any secrets."

"I wouldn't keep my secret from you," Mill replied.

"But you chose a stranger over me. You saw it as a polo opportunity that you would never be able to get otherwise, and broke up with me."

"For you," Mill revised.

"Oh, stuff it. It wasn't for me, none of it was."

"I thought..."

"That I would get over it?"

"Yes."

"Well, you were right. I did. Thanks. Don't come back here." Cap began walking toward the tack room.

Mill watched her go. "I'm going to be at Acadiana."

"So?" she asked without stopping.

"You want this separation to be permanent?"

I looked at Lockie.

"That's the general idea as I understood it," Cap called.

"It's over? After three years?"

90

"You broke up with me, so yes. I didn't run after my father begging for his approval and you should have figured it out that you weren't more special to me than he is."

"Caprice!" Mill shouted.

Cap appeared from the tack room. "No one treats me like this. Not even you, Millais." She exited from the rear door.

Mill strode past us on the way to his truck.

I sighed.

"Promise me something," Lockie said. "If I beg, give me another chance."

One glance and I could see how serious he was.

"Did you do this thing already?" I asked.

"No."

"Do you have any idea what this thing is going to be?"

"It would be a mistake, wouldn't it?"

"And it would make me really angry with you."

"Very."

I thought about how miserable we had all been when my mother wouldn't forgive my father. If she had been able to see into the future, know that the clock was ticking faster and something precious was being lost as the second hand progressed around the clock face, maybe that would have made her reconsider. But it wasn't until time had almost run out, that she recanted. What had she won? Even if the illness hadn't galloped over her more swiftly than the doctors could perform their arts, what was left behind was never to be reclaimed.

Spending those last months teaching me so much for the future we wouldn't share, my mother had no idea what I was learning from her.

"Talia. Tell me you'd give me another chance."

"Yes, of course I would."

He held me to him.

"Silly."

***

While we ate barbecued steaks, turned our faces into a buttery mess with corn, and filled the center of the table with used napkins, I got to know Wynne and Dan, and they got to know the whole sorry lot of us at the farm. There was Chartier Cajun Steak Sauce on every table and Teche applied it to his meat liberally. The smallest drop on my tongue had me grabbing for my water glass, but no one else seemed to mind.

Dessert was a selection of Unspeakably Desirable pastries, which were unspeakably delicious and in shapes I had never seen before. There were glossy chocolate covered pyramids, frosted spheres, and mousses of all varieties. The showstopper was a many-tiered cake decorated with our stable colors and pastillage bittersweet vines.

We ate until we couldn't take one more bite.

I leaned over to Jules. "Will you teach me how to make pastries like this?"

"Bel's a genius but we can start with the basics. I'm sure you have the time to devote to a buttercream intensive."

"We all need a hobby," I replied.

Jules laughed.

Squaring the Circle took the stage and began setting up their instruments. All the members were dressed like farmers in overalls or jeans and plaid shirts.

"I thought you were kidding," Lockie said to me.

"You wanted me to square dance so here we are."

"Leave me out of it," he replied.

"No way, mister. You'll do-si your do with me or have a good reason why you can't."

"I have two left feet."

"Almost everyone does. Come up with something else."

"The dance floor looks slippery."

"Non-slip surface. You can do better than that," I said.

"It's not slippery enough."

"It's a competition grade portable dance floor. Next."

"Do you have a rebuttal to everything I say?"

I nodded.

"Tali. I have to confess something."

"Is it the big thing?"

He looked at me in confusion, then remembered. "No. I've never square danced."

"None of us has." I thought for a moment. "Greer knows how to do all those dances from Jane Austen movies but only historic British dances. No American dances. That's why it's fun."

Lockie looked at me in disbelief.

"You bump into each other and laugh at your ineptitude."

"I don't want to publicize my ineptitudes. That's not amusing."

I was surprised. "You used to be fun."

"I reject that characterization," he replied.

"You must have been fun before you came here. When you were so popular on the show circuit."

Lockie leaned over to me. "I was popular because I was one of the very few straight men." He sat up. "Not a situation entirely without benefits."

"You're awful."

"I'm the opposite of awful. Just ask any of the girls I dated."

"Dated is the word for it now?"

"In polite company, yes, it is," Lockie replied. "Many times, that's all it was. Life is very different on the circuit if you get on, ride the class, and then leave for the on-going party of the day. I got up early, took care of the horses, coached my riders, rode, coached my riders, showed, took care of my horses, and was lucky if I got back to my room by midnight. That kind of schedule doesn't leave a lot of time for socializing even when it's very tempting to hand the reins over to a groom and have some of the fun everyone else is having."

I shook my head. "That doesn't sound believable. Don't forget, I was there. I saw it firsthand."

"You did not see what was going on firsthand. Be glad. I am."

The band began playing and the caller encouraged the guests to find a partner, and take the floor.

Lockie stood and held out his hand to me. "May I have this dance?"

"You may have all of them."

"Just one and then we can go home."

I nodded.

***

From our terrace, we could hear the sound of music and laughter. The tree toads were singing and summer was in the air.

"This is an ideal evening," I said.

We had stumbled around the dance floor, bumping into other couples, allemanding right when we should have been going left until Jules and I were doubled up with laughter and unable to dance another step. Lockie was correct. It was fun for that one time. With him.

Greer came around the corner of the house. "Can I stay with you tonight? Cam left with Kitty."

I sighed.

"I won't get in your way," she insisted.

Lockie laughed.

13

GREER AND I LEFT RIGHT AFTER CHORES in order to go to the tack shop. It was not that we were in desperate need of anything, although at any time, nearly anything was on the verge of breaking and a replacement should be bought. It was that Cam was going to be at the farm that morning and so was Kitty.

I wasn't sure how to talk to Greer about this issue. She didn't seem to be able to resolve it for herself but it had to come from her. Cam's feelings for Greer had been made quite plain to me at the Miry Brook Show even if he wouldn't admit them.

It seemed like such a simple step to take, to put her hand around his. No words were required. It wasn't as though he was going to drop her hand as if he had been burned.

But now, Greer was convinced there was something going on between Kitty and Cam. I thought she felt she had not acted soon enough, not acted before she was ready and now Kitty was there as an old friend and all that implied.

It was not difficult to understand why this would discomfort Greer but I believed Kitty was at the farm to solve her own problems—that of preparing for her first big event and having a horse who wasn't adhering to the training schedule.

I hadn't seen Nearkis go, so I had no idea what the resistance was but had the feeling that if the horse wasn't keeping to the timetable, adjust the timetable to the horse.

Of course, that was difficult to do as the season was moving right along, and there would be fewer events to attend as the autumn progressed. Event horses tended to take time off unlike hunters, jumpers and equitation horses who now were lucky to get a break of a few weeks between indoors and Florida.

"Did you dance at all last night?"

"Yes. Mr. Auerbach and I whirled around while Cam laughed."

"If he was laughing, I'm sure he was happy to see you enjoying yourself."

"I wasn't."

"You never had trouble going up to a guy before and being quite direct about what you wanted. If you wanted to dance with Cam, you should have asked him to dance with you."

"What if he didn't want to?"

"Then he would have thanked you for the offer but wanted to spend all his time with Greg, and we wouldn't have to be talking about it today."

"He left early with Kitty!"

"Her truck wasn't there this morning. How do you know they went some place together. Maybe he was just going home."

"Don't act like I don't know how these assignations work."

I shook my head. "I'm sure you do. What is patently clear is that you do not know how Cam works."

"If you were going to lecture me, why did you come along?"

"Because you insisted upon it. I had plenty to do at home, and I would ignore Kitty's training session with Lockie."

"So you're saying there is something to ignore!"

"No."

"Lockie's perfect, of course you have nothing to think about."

"No one is perfect but at least we talk to each other. If you talked to Cam about your relationship instead of me, maybe we wouldn't be shouting at each other now."

"That can be solved!"

We ran our errands and returned to the barn in silence. As soon as we parked, Poppy and Gincy ran out of the barn.

"You missed all the excitement."

"Just what my life lacks," Greer groaned.

"You know that horse on the television?"

I shook my head. "Can I buy a vowel?"

"The cowboy one," Gincy said.

"What channel is this?" Greer asked.

"Cowboy Channel," Poppy said.

"The horse gallops from way back there and then stands up."

Poppy nodded.

"A horse stood up?" Greer asked.

"Where's Lockie?" I asked.

"The hospital."

"I should never leave!" I turned toward my truck.

"No, Talia. Lockie's fine. The horse with the big teeth stood up and fell back..."

"Fell?" Greer headed into the barn.

Gincy looked up. "That woman, Cat?"

"Kitty," Poppy corrected, and continued, "hurt her arm so Lockie took her to the emergency room."

"Why didn't anyone call me?" I asked.

Gincy shrugged.

Feeling as though I was totally out of the loop, I went into the barn and headed to the sound of running water. Cap was hosing down the mare's hind leg.

"She scuffed it up pretty well but I don't know that she did any real damage. Dr. Fortier's on the way to make sure."

When I took a step closer to check on the leg, the mare put her ears back.

"She's really in a bad mood," I said.

"If you fell, you'd be pretty unhappy, too."

"What were they doing when she reared," Greer asked.

"I wasn't watching," Cap answered. "What I was told is that they were training over that bounce gymnastic out there. She did it once and quit. When Kitty asked her to go forward, she reared. Unfortunately, the mare lost her balance."

"She was really standing up."

Cap nodded. "Kitty fell on her arm. I grabbed the horse and they went to the hospital."

"Kitty's lucky the horse didn't fall on her," I said.

"That happened at Robert Easton's," Poppy started.

"I'm sure it did."

"He yelled at the girl for not kicking the horse forward," Gincy added. "I was scared."

"I would have been, too," I agreed.

"Dr. Fortier's here," Greer said as she went to the doorway. "I have no idea what we're going to say. Where's Cam? Wasn't he here when the accident happened?"

Cap turned off the water. "By then, he and the Ruhlmanns already left to go look at some horses at Acadiana."

"You can explain it to Dr. Fortier," I said to Cap.

"I didn't see it happen either. I was grooming Bijou when Poppy ran in."

As much as I liked the Zuckerlumpens, they saw the horse stand up and that was about it. We weren't going to learn anything more than that.

Dr. Fortier came down the aisle, greeted us, and began to look at the mare's leg. "I think you know she has a bruise and that's about it. Why am I here?"

"This is supposed to be a very nice horse," I said.

"She is," Dr. Fortier agreed.

"Who nipped Gincy yesterday."

Gincy held out her arm as proof.

"Today, out of character, she rears and falls," I replied.

Dr. Fortier was examining the mare. "And you think what?"

"Is there a medical reason for the personality change?"

"She's not in heat," he said.

Greer shrugged as if that ended the discussion.

When he began pressing her belly, the mare squealed and struck out with her front hoof. Greer managed to grab Poppy and pull her out of the way just in time.

"Okay," Dr. Fortier said, stepping back. "Bring her up to the office and we'll run some tests."

"Like?"

"An ultrasound to start. Maybe there's something going on that we can't see. Has she been eating and drinking normally?"

"It couldn't be colic, could it?"

"Bring her in and we'll find out. Let's not borrow trouble," Dr. Fortier cautioned. "Where's the owner?"

"At the hospital. She got hurt when she hit the ground."

Dr. Fortier patted her. "You are creating quite a bit of drama, aren't you?"

She put her ears back in response.

"Yes, you are." He gathered his things together. "Be careful transporting her. She's not in a very good mood. Is Lockie around?"

We walked him to his truck.

"He took Kitty to the hospital."

"Be alert. Take precautions." Dr. Fortier opened the truck door. "I'll let them know you'll be there. I doubt if we'll know anything today so don't expect an answer soon."

"I could be nothing," Greer said.

"Sure. It could be." He sat down. "We'll run tests and know more. Have a good afternoon."

"Thank you. You, too."

Greer and I watched him drive to the road and turn left.

"Why hasn't Lockie called?"

"You can't always use a phone in the hospital," Greer replied.

"He can't walk outside?"

"Maybe he can't leave her," Greer said.

"Why would that be?"

"Maybe she doesn't want him to leave her. Moral support. I don't know. We'll put her in his trailer instead of the van."

I nodded. I didn't want any trouble with the mare going up the ramp.

"Now or after lunch?"

"If we do it now, we have most of the afternoon left. If we wait, we won't have time to do anything."

We were turning to go back into the barn when Cam's truck came down the drive and parked next to us.

He got out. "Lockie called."

"He called you and not me?"

"Yes, he has a crush on me since we square danced together by mistake."

I remembered the time all the couples being switched and lost to each other in the crowd.

"I'm really his type. He likes girls with facial hair. Sheesh, Tal. There's some kind of phone outage, a tower is down. What's the crisis here?"

"Kitty horse reared and fell."

"I know that. What did the vet say?"

"He wants her brought to the office so they can run tests like an ultrasound."

"Lockie thought it would be more than a barn call. Get his truck and trailer backed up to the door and I'll load her."

"We can load her," Greer said.

Cam shook his head. "Lockie asked me to do it. He saw the horse. He was there when it happened. Let's just take his word for it."

We headed for Lockie's rig while Cam went to get the mare ready for her journey. A few minutes later, I was lowering the ramp so the mare could go right from the barn into the trailer.

Nearkis danced down the aisle but under Cam's control. He led her into the trailer and we lifted the ramp quickly.

It was as though her personality had changed completely. When she arrived she was quiet and relaxed, today she was dangerous.

Cam exited from the trailer. "Who's going with me?"

Greer and I looked at each other.

"If something happens on the way I'll need help." He got into the driver's side. "Someone get in the truck!"

I pushed Greer. "Go. I'll stay here and wait for Lockie. Call me when you get there. If you can."

Greer ran to the passenger side and jumped in just as Cam was starting to pull away.

The mare's hoofs banged against the trailer until it was out of sight.

Cap stepped up alongside me. "So was that Greer kicking the floorboards of the pickup?"

"I'm glad you haven't lost your sense of humor," I replied.

"I'm okay. I—" Cap sighed. "Mill knows me better than that, or at least I thought he did. That's what's upsetting. He broke up with me and expected, once he came back, I would be understanding. I'm not. I understand but that's not enough."

"You have your life experiences and those are your guiding principles."

"You wouldn't like to tell me to work it out with him?"

"It has nothing to do with me. You have a good job, I hope you think it's a good job," I said.

"I do."

"You're back in your hometown. You have a place for Bijou. You have a nice horse to ride and a show to prepare for so will you ride in with the Zucks this afternoon?"

"Sure."

I started to turn, then stopped. "Thanks, Cap."

"For what?"

"For having a good attitude no matter what. Better than me, sometimes."

"Not true," Cap replied.

"I won't argue with you but just consider us glad to have you here."

"I appreciate that. Especially now."

"All change requires incorporating it into your life and that's not always easy but it happens eventually."

Cap nodded.

"Put neckstraps on all the horses and ponies riding in the lesson," I said.

Cap groaned.

I shrugged.

***

We were working without stirrups and their reins knotted onto their mounts' necks while going over a low gymnastic. It took strength and balance. The neckstrap was there so they didn't grab the reins if they felt insecure. The point was to develop an independent seat and hanging onto the reins would never help them achieve that.

Tighter in the saddle than ever before, Gincy was catching up to Poppy. It wouldn't surprise me to have Gincy and Beau giving Poppy and Tango real competition at the show.

The show at Pickwick Farm was larger than they had gone to before, but it was close, and since the goal for us was never about ribbons but about gaining experience, I was happy to have them ride in with more ponies. The fences would be attractive and well-built, so I was sure we'd all enjoy the day.

Cap would ride Spare in a few jumper classes and Buck was supposed to show Wingspread in the junior hunter division. Since I hadn't heard from him since before the holiday, I wasn't sure what his plans were. Buck was a strong enough rider so that he wouldn't be negatively impacted by having a week off, but I could think of a handful of things that would have done him some good instead of staying away.

Day Jamieson was still in Canada fishing at a remote lake in Northern Ontario with her grandmother. They took a vacation each year before the cubbing season started, so Moonie was getting to act like a pasture pet for a few weeks.

At the head of the line, Gincy used the reins to point Beau at the fences, then let them rest on his neck.

"Gincy, let Beau jump up to you and steer with your legs. Don't let him drift."

I knew how difficult this was for her as Gincy was just beginning to achieve some coordination, but the improvement over the past few months had made me so proud of her.

"Look up, Poppy," I called as Tango began to trot down the side of the ring. "He's still there, you don't need to check to make sure."

Spare followed the ponies. "Cap, don't let your lower leg slip back. You're pinching with your knee. If you do this over a little bounce, what are you going to do over a big fence?"

Cap closed her calf on Spare's sides.

"Perfect! Everyone walk and relax for a minute."

As I began to reset the height of the last two elements, I saw Kitty's truck pull into the yard and Lockie got out. No Kitty. That wasn't a good sign.

"Okay, gang, the fences are a little higher. What does that mean?"

They looked at me. No one answered.

"You don't need to do more. I want you to trust your horse. Pay attention to your position and let the horse go forward under you."

Cap looked at me.

"Really," I said to her. "What's the worst that can happen?"

Cap regarded with me in disbelief.

"No one is going to fall off. The worst that will happen is that you'll knock down a rail. Let your horse take care of you."

"Are you sure about this?" Lockie said softly into my ear.

"Of course," I replied. "They're not going to have confidence if every time they ride, they feel like they have to multitask. It's a partnership. You imagine the horse will either not know how to get over the fence without your input or that he'll take advantage of you. Not true."

"Do I think that?" Lockie asked.

109

"With CB you do."

Lockie thought for a moment.

"Okay, ladies. Are we ready? Legs firmly against your horse's sides, position him in front of the gymnastic and let fate take over."

"Fate?" Gincy called back to me.

"Head up! Back flat. Arms out to the side."

Each of the riders made it through the gymnastic with no difficulty even though they let their horses set their own pace. I was especially glad to see Beau work it out for himself.

"That was lovely. You've had enough for today, you can go for a hack."

"May we have our stirrups back," Poppy asked.

"Next time." I smiled.

Lockie opened the gate for them and the three headed toward the field where the tent was being removed.

14

WE STARTED back to the barn.

"I'm afraid to ask. How is Kitty?"

"The doctor says she broke her wrist and they gave her some painkillers that made her sleepy. I left her at the inn."

"Should she be alone? She could have stayed here," I said. "We should call in a few hours and offer."

He leaned over and kissed my cheek. "Thank you."

***

I spotted Lockie on Kyff in the indoor, although most of the work was on the flat. Kyff's first reaction to anything new was to become anxious and tense. We had to traverse a very narrow path to keep progressing without giving him more than he could mentally handle.

It was obvious he had been rushed from the first moment someone had gotten on him. Time is money and Kyff looked like a lot of potential money in the bank. Whoever had gotten him just wanted to make the sale and let the next trainer undo the emotional damage. That trainer said the same thing. Everyone said the same thing until Kyff came to us.

By next year, he would be relaxed about doing his job. Right now, he wasn't.

"How do I look?" Lockie asked as he cantered slowly around me in a twenty-meter circle.

"What do you mean?"

"If you were giving me a lesson."

As if that would ever happen. "You're perfect."

"No one is perfect."

"Is this a test?"

"For who? You or me?"

Kyff did a flying change and they went in the other direction.

"I want you to see what's in front of you."

"It is a test."

"Yes. You need to see me with different eyes."

"I don't know what you mean."

"You see me as your trainer."

"Yes, because you are."

Lockie sat back and Kyff walked. "But I'm not perfect, and I intentionally made mistakes that you didn't see. Not because you're not capable of analyzing my ride, it's because your expectations cloud your vision. You see everything with your pony riders."

"I see everything for their level. Since you are many levels above me, it would be ridiculous for me to comment."

"Talia, that's not true. There are subtleties you have not yet learned, but that doesn't mean you can't judge the overall performance."

"You just did a change of lead seamlessly. There was nothing to see."

"You must be as critical of me as you would be of any rider."

I shook my head. "I don't want to."

"You won't hurt my feelings. You need to gain the confidence to be able to understand and verbalize what you're seeing. I know you sense it. Every once in a while, you say something without realizing it. Do it consciously. Think. Intellectualize your riding and teaching, don't just go by instinct."

"There's so much I don't know and so much you do."

"Then when you're working with me and you see something, phrase it as a question. Ask and we'll discuss it."

For Lockie, riding was not only a physical exercise it was a mental exercise. All of it challenged him.

"You've been here a year. I've watched you ride, we've talked, and I think I know you pretty well."

"I agree."

"You have something I don't and that's the drive to excel. You have been blessed with a body that's ideal for riding. You have the right temperament. Many people have those gifts, but you have the trifecta. You're keen on competing. You'll do it against other riders or you'll do it against yourself. You push and you grow. I don't care about competing. I just want to do right by the horses."

"Isn't that your own trifecta?"

"That's not a quality missing in you."

"If I have all your gifts and more, why does CB give me such a hard time?"

"When I look at him, he is perfection. He knows that's how I feel about him. When you go to ride CB, he's the next horse on your schedule. He knows that. Everyone wants to feel approval and valued. No one wants to feel anonymous."

"How does CB know this?"

"It's so obvious. I kiss him, I rub his ears, I sing to him. You tack him up and get on. When you're done, you give him a perfunctory pat."

"I drink with him. We have beers together like a couple of guys."

"When's the last time you did that?"

"A while."

"That's okay. We forgive you every time we share a hard cider."

"Miss Margolin. You're not supposed to be drinking."

"I just pretend for his sake."

Lockie laughed. "He doesn't want to drink alone?"

"He doesn't."

Sliding off Kyff, Lockie ran up the irons. "This empathy is your gift. Don't make light of it. Maybe it's something you can teach me. Do you think that's possible?"

He held out his arm and I stepped into the space he made for me.

***

When Lockie's phone rang, it was so late in the afternoon, that the sky was beginning to turn peach-colored at the edges.

Cam and Greer hadn't returned from the vet clinic. Cap was out with a friend from Old Newbury and Kitty was sleeping off the meds the doctor had given her.

My father had gone to a business dinner with the serious men who had been hanging around for days. Jules had gone along because Trevillian was one of the most exclusive restaurants in the Northeast and sampling menus was endlessly entertaining to her. I imagined the food would be far more fascinating than the conversation but Jules assured me she would be taking notes and tell me all about it.

I left Lockie to his conversation and began turning the horses out for the night, CB with Kyff and Henry, Wingspread with Greer's colt and Jetzt. It was a never-ending process making sure every horse had equal access to the pastures.

The ground was becoming dry and hard from lack of rain, which meant the grass wasn't growing the way we needed. The prediction was for rain in time for the horse show, of course.

"That was interesting," Lockie said as I returned to the barn.

"Who was it?"

"The Bouley's lawyer."

"Not again," I replied. "The grandmother is on the warpath?"

"No, she won."

"How did she do that?"

"She bought him a farm. The lawyer offered me a quarter of a million dollars for Wing so Buck has an event horse ready to go."

"You're not serious."

Lockie nodded.

"Who's his trainer?"

"I wasn't told."

"Where's the farm?"

"Down the road from the family estate. I was assured this was Buck's choice."

I didn't even need to think about it. "She bought him."

"I would say so," Lockie replied with a shrug. "That's how rich people get their own way. They raise the price until you can't say no. Let's finish up here and go home."

"Are you considering selling Wing?"

That was a staggering amount of money for a horse who really hadn't done anything in competition yet. If Wing went down the road, it would be easy enough for Lockie to leave and start his own business. He wouldn't be the first trainer who financed a farm with their attractive horse.

"No. Why would I?"

"The money?"

"Not everyone has a price."

I hadn't actually found that to be true. At school, money had been the motivating factor for most students whether they came from a financially stable family or not. If they had money, they wanted more, or their own. If they didn't have money, they thought having it would buy their way into the elite circle other students inhabited so adroitly.

The A show circuit was a rich people's sport. My father always put us on a budget, a generous one to be sure, he wanted us competitive, but it had not been unlimited. When equitation horses could cost a half a million dollars, I was on Butch. Trying so hard to make it that one more step to the blue instead of the red, Greer sold Tea Biscuit and found Sans Egal, who didn't do one whit better for her ribbon-wise, and they never connected emotionally.

117

This point of balance seemed to be where we were happiest. CB was a bad boy and Tea was plain. They were loved for who they were, not for the shine they could put on our egos.

"You should only keep Wing if he means something to you," I said.

"He does," Lockie replied. "You gave him to me."

"Let's go home and find something to eat."

***

Lockie put together the salad Jules had left for us while I sliced the grilled chicken, and spooned faro with mushrooms onto plates. Then we brought everything out onto our terrace and ate while watching the horses graze.

As we started on dessert of chocolate-dipped hazelnut shortbread cookies that were somehow left over from the party, Greer arrived.

"Did you go out to eat?" I asked.

"No. Is there anything here?"

"Yes, it's in the refrigerator."

"Where's Cam?" Lockie asked.

"Parking your rig," she replied sharply, entering the house.

"Were we like this?" Lockie asked me softly so Greer wouldn't hear.

I shook my head as Greer returned with a plate.

"You were at the vet's the whole time?" I asked.

"Yes."

"What's wrong with the mare?"

"Dr. Fortier ran tests and needs to run more tomorrow. It's nothing simple."

Lockie finished his cookie then reached for another. "Do they have any idea?"

"It's serious enough to cause a personality disruption," Greer replied.

I glanced across the table to him. "What a mess. Kitty brought the horse up here to train, falls off the first day and the horse has something more dramatic wrong with her than she doesn't like the view from her stall."

"And there's Buck," Lockie added.

"What about Buck?" Cam asked coming around the side of the house.

"The grandmother bought him a farm," I said. "The lawyer offered Lockie a quarter of a million dollars for Wing, so he wouldn't have to develop an event horse from scratch."

Cam turned and went back around to the front of the house. A moment later, he returned. "He lived with us, but he couldn't call so I wouldn't have to read about it in *The Chronicle*."

"He's sixteen," I said.

"When I was sixteen I was dealing with producers, agents, other actors and riding the circuit. I wasn't afraid to pick up the damn phone."

"You had all the advantages a child could ask for," I replied. "Your parents love you."

"Isn't that a sentiment from a faded Mother's Day card dug out of the dusty back rack at Wilbon's Pharmacy," Greer shot back.

"Now I know where Victoria got her way with words," Cam replied. "She inherited the ability from you."

"Enough," Lockie said. "Buck's gone. He made his choice. His grandmother is happy. The father can go back to Singapore or wherever he was. We have to deal with Kitty's injury and her horse. Since we can't do anything about that tonight—"

"Cam, would you like some dinner? There's plenty," I offered.

"No, thank you, I'll head home. To the dusty Mother's Day card recipient."

"I didn't say Kate." Greer dropped her fork onto the plate with a loud clatter. "You're making it seem as though I'm insulting her and that wasn't my intention."

"This is like a *Rocky* movie. Ding. Ding. Ding. Go to your corners," I said.

"I'll be at Acadiana tomorrow if you need me," Cam said. "Have a good night." He walked around the front of the house and a moment later, we heard his truck leave.

Greer pushed her plate away then stood. "I don't know how to talk to him."

"Did you fight with him the whole time?"

She gave me a look. "Yes."

"About what?" Lockie asked.

"I don't know."

"I'm going in. You two can work it out, if possible." Lockie went into the house.

"May I stay here tonight?"

I didn't answer.

"No one's home."

"Yes."

***

"How long is she going to cry?" Lockie asked after he turned off the light.

"Until there are no more tears."

"Will she get dehydrated?"

I laughed.

He snuggled closer. "Living with girls is a lot different than living with boys."

"Better or worse?"

"Mysterious," he whispered.

15

I WAS WATCHING GINCY AND POPPY jump pony-sized fences in the ring just after nine when my phone rang.

"Hi, Dr. Fortier."

"Hi, Talia. Here's the diagnosis with the mare. We strongly suspect she has a granulosa cell. That would be an ovarian tumor."

"Geez. That sounds serious. I don't know what I thought it would be, but nothing like that."

"It's a horse, they're large animals. The tumor could be thirty or forty pounds."

"Poor thing!" I replied.

"Yes. She's probably in quite a bit of pain and that's why she's been acting out."

"What can be done?"

"I called Tufts and they'll assess her and do the surgery. It's too complicated for the clinic."

"Okay. So we need to get her there."

"As soon as possible," Dr. Fortier said. "Today, tomorrow. Not next week."

"I understand. It's an emergency."

"It is. She'll be recovering for months. I make no guarantees as to her future competitive abilities. I know she's not your horse, but explain that to the owner."

"I'm sure Kitty just wants her to get well and be comfortable. I'll make the arrangements for transportation and get back to you with the details."

"Fine. And Talia, worrying won't help."

"I'm so predictable."

"Yes, but it a good way. Talk to you later."

"I'll get right on it. Bye."

I clicked off the phone and stood there for a moment, trying to sort through all the information.

Greer couldn't go all the way to Massachusetts with Cam. They needed a time out. Kitty would be of no help because of her wrist in a cast. We needed Cap. We needed Lockie.

Freddi and Cam.

I noticed Poppy and Gincy had stopped and were in front of me.

"What's wrong, Talia?" Poppy asked.

"Nearkis needs special surgery and has to go to Tufts University where they will take good care of her."

"Was that why she bit me?" Gincy asked.

"You're a smart girl. It could have been the reason. That's a reminder for us to never blame bad acts on bad temperament first without knowing more about the horse. They could be in pain."

"Or scared," Poppy added.

"That's right. I would like you to go to the stream, let the ponies have a drink and walk back. Then Cap will help you get ready for the show tomorrow. Is that good for you?"

They nodded and while they headed up the driveway, I went into the lower barn to see if Greer was in her office and she was.

"I got a call from Dr. Fortier and Nearkis needs a ride to Tufts."

Greer looked up. "Do you want me to go?"

"I'm going to ask Cam and Freddi."

"Why Freddi?"

"Because you and Cam need a time out. He's going to a show tomorrow—"

"Long River," Greer supplied.

"Yes. That gives you a few days away from each other and time to think."

"I've thought."

"Good. With Freddi gone for the rest of the day, I'm going to need some help getting the ponies ready. Cap's riding Spare so she has her own work to do."

Greer nodded.

"Where's Lockie?"

"He left for town to pick up Kitty, they should be back soon."

"Okay. So after lunch you're free?"

"Yes."

On the way to the house, I called Cam and explained the situation to him. He agreed to drive Nearkis to Tufts as soon as he had taken care of everything for Long River.

I entered the kitchen and found Jules making some cole slaw, obviously for my grandfather who loved it.

"Tea," I said.

"To drink or the horse?" Jules asked, whisking the eggs to make mayonnaise.

"Drink."

"Hot or cold?"

"Is there hot water? I need fortifying."

Jules pointed to the kettle. "What happened?"

"Everything." I poured a mug of water and searched in the jar for my favorite tea bags.

"Can you narrow it down a little?"

"Kitty's horse needs specialized surgery that only can be performed at a top flight veterinary hospital. So the day before everyone is going to a horse show, someone has to run that horse up to Tufts."

"That someone being Cam, I assume," Jules replied.

I nodded as I sipped the brewed tea.

"It's serious."

I nodded again and reached for a cookie.

"Don't spoil your lunch."

"In scientific studies, has it been proven that having a nosh spoils your appetite?" I asked.

"I'm just repeating what my mother used to say to me."

"An old wives' tale, then?"

"If eating before the meal spoiled your appetite, appetizers wouldn't have been invented, would they?"

I smiled. "You're so clever, but you haven't told me about the meal last night."

"Grim," Jules replied. "I thought it was possible to have dinner without talking politics but I was wrong. They are giving your father the hard sell."

"Did you get a sense of where he is on this election?"

"He was very polite and more attentive than I would have been."

"My father has manners," I said. "Unlike his wolf cub children."

Jules laughed. "That's not true. You're always lovely with me."

"That's because you get the special family dispensation. Outsiders, not so much."

The door opened. Lockie and Kitty entered.

"I've been waiting for you to get back. Cam will be here in a while to take Nearkis to Tufts. It's a gran...I don't remember the medical term, ovarian tumor, they think."

Kitty drew a breath. "Are they sure? Should we get a second opinion?"

"It didn't seem as though there was time to think about it, just act."

"I should go with Cam."

"You'd be no help," Lockie said, reasonably.

"Moral support. I should stay there with her." Kitty turned around. "It's a good thing I packed a bag. I can rent a car there."

"Are you able to drive?" Jules asked.

"I'll manage." She held up her arm. "It's not that bad. I have the use of my fingers."

"Let me pack some food." Jules went into high gear to make sandwiches.

"Thank you," Kitty said. "Where's the ladies room? It's going to be a long drive."

"Down the hall on the right," I replied.

Kitty left the kitchen and I crossed to the door. "I'll wait for Cam and you can be with Kitty so she doesn't feel alone."

Lockie smiled reassuringly. "She'll be okay."

Leaving the house, I wondered how everyone was going to deal with the crisis. The trip would take several hours, and the mare had not been happy on the short drive to the vet. A little something to calm her down wouldn't be ruled out, I hoped.

I wished there was something we could give Greer to calm her down. Extra strength chamomile tea might work.

When I reached the barn, Poppy was helping Gincy wash Beau and then they would do Tango. I liked seeing them able to help each other and have fun with the work.

Greer and I had never been as lighthearted the day before a show. There was so much pressure on both of us. Different for each but equally as life-threatening, it seemed.

I didn't want to be in any way similar to the trainers we had suffered with. Each of them had been a wrong match in their own way. Some of them could ride but not teach. Others didn't seem to know much about riding or teaching. Others didn't seem to want to teach at all but use the position as a steppingstone to something more glamorous and financially rewarding.

There had been one young woman who had been fun, at least I had thought so. Dee didn't take any of it too seriously, smiling and laughing during lessons. That upset Greer who couldn't relax for a moment. Even if she won, it wasn't good enough.

Dee wasn't Lockie. It was true she was just a rider a half dozen years older than we were, but she did know more than we did and had ridden at all the major shows as a junior. She lasted about six months and I was very sorry to see her go. Greer was not unhappy in the least. But it was all downhill from Dee. Until Lockie.

Those years had taught me what kind of trainer I did not want to be. If my horses were uncomfortable, if my riders were nervous, I was failing.

Winning a blue ribbon wasn't a Good Horsekeeping Seal of Approval. It wasn't a Life Merit Badge. It was just a pretty length of ribbon.

"Cam's here," Cap called from the doorway.

I walked up the aisle and found him getting out of his truck. "Thanks."

"No problem. Are we ready to go, because I have a show tomorrow and have to get back."

"The truck is gassed. Freddi's going along to help and stop at the house to pick up Kitty."

Cam nodded as we crossed to Lockie's rig.

"I want to apologize for Greer's behavior."

He opened the driver's side door and got in. "Why?"

"All the fighting..."

"I love to fight with Greer. It's like sex without the touching."

I stared at him.

"You don't fight with Lockie?"

"No."

Cam laughed. "Try it. You might like it."

Freddi ran to the truck from the barn, threw her duffel bag in the back, and got in.

"See you later," he said, and started up the drive.

I returned to the barn and found Cap in the tack room. "I hope this isn't being nosey, but I have a question."

"Shoot."

"Did you fight with Mill? Before you broke up."

"Yes. Now that I look back on it, I'm not surprised at all that it didn't work out."

"Cap!" Gincy called. "Beau's standing on the hose and we can't get him off!"

Cap shrugged and went to help the girls.

Since I still hadn't had lunch, I started toward the house and met Lockie coming down to the barn.

"Do you have time for a session on CB," he asked.

"Why?"

"Because I want to see you ride him."

"Did you eat? Because I haven't."

"After we eat, then yes?"

"Yes. Let me ask you a question."

He thought for a moment. "No. I never like it when it starts like that."

"I'm asking anyway."

"That's predictable."

"Do you think we would have a better relationship if we argued?"

"Do you?"

"No."

Walking in silence until we reached the terrace, I stopped.

"What would we argue about?"

"Tch. How you don't take care of yourself!" I replied.

"You shouldn't worry about me so much."

"I have to."

"Okay then. Are we done arguing?"

"I guess so."

"Was it as good for you as it was for me?"

I shrugged. "It was nothing."

"Exactly."

16

WHILE GINCY AND POPPY were washing Tango and Greer was braiding Beau's tail, I rode CB in the indoor. After warming up, we did some leg yields, shoulder-ins and a half pass, then I reined back to a walk.

"What do you want us to do?"

"I just want to watch. Do what you would normally do."

I dropped my reins to the buckle.

"Why is that what you would normally do?"

"It's a summer afternoon. Neither of us wants to work."

"How do you know he doesn't want to work?

"Look at his ears. He's not moving away from my leg the way he would if he was enthusiastic. I think he wants to go back to his stall and lay down for a while."

"Talia, please."

"The fan blowing air on him. It will be very pleasant." I stroked his neck.

"We don't get to choose the weather. We have our chores to do whether it's hot or cold or raining. We don't ask a lot from them in return, just a little cooperation."

"I understand that but he's a horse and what he knows is that he left hay in his stall in order to go around in circles."

"Are you trying to make a point?" Lockie asked.

"If forced, I will. I think you could be more diplomatic with him. I don't understand...you already know the material and he already knows it. Why do you have to keep drilling him?"

"Athletes practice. The more you practice the better you get."

"He's telling you he doesn't want to practice."

"You're saying he's sour?"

"I wouldn't call it that. He's being quite a gentleman about it but you're not picking up the clues."

Lockie shook his head.

"Why can't you do in it smaller increments? Why can't you make it more fun for him?"

"This is not how it works."

I slid off. "And your way of how it works has been so successful with him?"

"If Henry was a better dressage horse, I would..."

I ran up my irons. "I know this is important to you. Try to accommodate him and I think he'll respond, but maybe not ever in the way you want. Maybe you need to find a dressage prospect that hasn't been spoiled or mistreated."

CB frisked my pocket for the cookies he could smell there, so I took one out and offered it to him.

"It will take years to get a green horse to CB's level."

"I understand. You're not going to take shortcuts, like they tried to do with CB. He's being pretty nice about it. Meet him half-way."

Lockie started walking out of the indoor.

"Don't be discouraged with him. He'll sense that."

A half hour later, after I had given him a little bath and CB smelled of Bigeloil, Lockie and I were walking past CB's stall and looked inside. He was stretched out on the bedding sound asleep.

"I'm in an alternate universe," Lockie said as we left the barn.

I took his hand. "But I'm in that universe with you."

"You're not my problem." He leaned over and pressed his lips against my cheek.

17

IT WAS DRIZZLING when we left for Pickwick Farm. By the time we arrived, it was raining. Greer and I had on our duster length raincoats and rubber Wellies. I already had my speech planned for suggesting we leave during the lunch break. The ponies would have a couple classes but Cap had decided to leave Spare at home because of the weather.

Lockie had decided to go horse hunting in Massachusetts with Dan and then swing by Long River and catch Cam in his jumper stake competition. It was just as well. Most of the time he would be in the truck or a barn, instead of dripping with rain the way we were.

"This is awful." Cap came up alongside us.

135

"Do I need to try to persuade everyone to leave at lunch?"

"Sweeten the deal a little," she replied.

"Chinese or pizza," Greer said.

"Pizza but at Antonio's. I want the cheese to be bubbling."

"Deal," Greer replied.

"It's probably better anyway. Robert Easton is here."

"Figures," I said.

"With Ami Gish."

"I suppose it was too much to ask to imagine we saw the last of her," Greer replied.

"I have nothing against her," I said. "I don't even have anything against Robert Easton."

"How did you manage to get those words out of your mouth?"

"Well, Greer, we're all grown-ups now."

She made a face at me.

"I'm an adult, then. It's a fact of life that he has a barn in the same state and we're bound to cross paths once in a while." I leaned over to Cap. "Remind me to show in New York State from now on."

Our first class was pony hunter under saddle. It would be easy to think that would be simple enough. Walk in, trot around the ring twice, canter around the ring twice, walk, rinse, repeat, pin the class and we're done with that.

Since it was a modest show, there were no subdivisions of ponies. Into the ring went the expected menagerie of ponies in all shapes and sizes. There were medium ones and little ones getting in the way of the bigger ones.

"People do this for a living, did you know that?" Greer asked.

"Oh, yes, I know that."

"You know that. And you still brought us here."

"Five dollars says someone gets run away with," Cap said.

"That's not a bet, that's a given," Greer replied. "I'm in if it's before they canter."

"It'll happen when they canter," Cap protested.

"Don't bet with her," I said. "She's banned at every casino in the South of France. She's a card counter."

Greer nodded with pride.

"How about a tack malfunction?"

"A tack malfunction and I'll raise you a someone-gets-kicked."

"I don't know who you people are," I said, taking a step to the side and bumping into the umbrella of Aly Beck.

"Hi, Tal. Does it always rain the day of a show?" Aly asked, moving the umbrella so I was under it.

"Oh, no. Sometimes it's below freezing."

She laughed.

Robert Easton was standing directly across from us on the other side of the ring, coaching all his riders as they went past.

My belief was that once the competitor entered the ring, it was too late for an extra lesson. Not everyone agreed with me, but it was how I worked and the Zuckerlumpens knew that.

To my surprise, Gincy pulled Beau up near me. "Ami's here."

"I know. Ignore her."

Ami had not been particularly kind to Gincy when they had ridden together even though Gincy was a far better rider. I understood how Ami's presence would distract Gincy.

"She's riding Oneco."

Oneco was Easton's unbeatable bay show pony with four white socks, owned by a syndicate, and he reminded me of so many other astronomically expensive horses we had competed against.

This was not a lesson I wanted Gincy to learn today. Easton used calmatives on all his horses. I didn't think any of his students had shown a horse that wasn't tuned down for their riding and winning pleasure.

On the other hand, I refused to lunge a horse before a class. By the time, we arrived at the showgrounds, it was too late to train the horse to do his job calmly. If he couldn't, we didn't belong there.

I was in the minority. I knew that.

I wasn't playing the horse show game as the rules were set out, never had. Somehow, I had to make this a positive experience for my girls.

"And you're riding your best friend. Get a good spot on the rail and stay there."

Maybe we should have brought Fudge who was just as fine a pony as Oneco, but that was also the wrong lesson. It suggested that it didn't matter how well they rode, the judge was going to pin the typiest pony.

That was going to be true anyway, just as it had been for me and Butch, and Greer and Tea riding against Nicole Boisvert on the Chick horse. I had to make sure my riders didn't leave the showgrounds feeling like failures the way Greer and I had.

"Some people enjoy showing," I said to no one in particular.

"Lockie does," Greer replied.

He did. Why? "His experience of it is not the same as ours."

"Give it a rest, Talia."

"I don't know what you mean."

Greer sighed in exasperation. "This means nothing to us. It's an activity. We will never have to earn a living doing this."

"That's the definition of sport. It's not a business," Cap added.

"But it is a business, even for us. Lockie works very diligently to make sure all our bills are paid."

"He doesn't have to work that hard. We can dial it back. We'll still train horses and riders. Winning isn't what we sell. Our business is built around creating happy athletes."

I nodded. "I shouldn't go to shows. I get confused."

The ponies were trotting.

"Stop holding your breath." Greer poked me in the side with her elbow.

They were asked to walk, then canter. It looked like the Oklahoma land rush, with large ponies overtaking the small ones. A little pony kicked out when someone got too close.

"Where's my tack malfunction?" Cap exclaimed.

Poppy was cut off at the top of the ring, and Tango broke into a trot for two strides before getting back to his canter.

"That's too bad," Aly said.

"One of the problems is cleaning the tack the day before a show. I clean but I don't soap. Too slippery." I pointed at a chestnut pony. "That rider just had her reins slip through her hands."

"Does that qualify as a tack malfunction?" Cap asked.

"No, something has to break or fall off," Greer replied. "Oo, watch it!"

Two ponies bumped shoulders across from us. The ringmaster saw it and asked for everyone to walk, then reverse.

"Not bad," I said.

Cap nodded. "Ami looks okay for someone who's scared to death."

"She's not what I would call a natural rider," Greer added.

"Why does her father want her to ride?"

"The same reason he forces her to take piano lessons. It's a good skill for later in life."

"Some parents are weird," Aly said. "But then my daughter would refuse to do anything she didn't want to do, so I'd be left taking the piano lessons."

"Poppy knows your love is not contingent on her performance."

"Thank you, Talia, that was very nice of you to say."

As one of his riders walked past, Robert Easton's coaching was so loud that everyone could hear.

"The riders need to wear a headset with earbuds," Cap said. "This is so hard! Going out into a showring and riding on your own. How unfair."

Greer nodded. "It would be much better to have the coaches talking in a soft voice into a mic, instead of shouting instructions from the rail. No one knows who's being criticized? 'Are my heels down enough or not?'"

"Maybe trainers shouldn't even come to the show. Would that be okay with you, Aly?" I asked.

"If you want to try it, I'm game."

"You'd be a nervous wreck back home," Cap pointed out.

"That's true," I admitted. "At least I'm fairly relaxed here."

The ponies were trotting past. Gincy had found herself a spot on the rail and was staying there. Beau was going at his normal speed, just a click too slow but I would rather have that and for them to be comfortable, than to push it in bad weather.

This was about experience, and experience told me to stay home on days like this, but the girls overruled me. Next time the forecast was for rain, maybe they would choose differently.

The ringmaster asked for everyone to walk. That took a bit more time than expected, since two ponies were very enthusiastic about trotting forcefully around. Once they were under control, the riders were asked to canter.

Both Gincy and Poppy got their correct lead immediately and settled into a nice, sedate canter. All our dressage work was paying off.

Twice around and the class was done.

18

ROBERT EASTON'S THREE RIDERS were pinned first, second and third, with Ami coming in second. There were whoops of joy from across the ring. Gincy was fourth and Poppy was fifth. Probably the judge took a couple points off for the break in the first canter. Cap whistled loudly. Greer applauded like the lady she was.

My phone rang as we walked back to the van. I looked at it. Lockie.

"Hi."

"How many empty stalls do we have?"

"Technically, none."

"Nearkis is gone."

"That's Keynote's stall."

"He can stay out."

"How many horses are you planning on bringing home?"

"Three. But one I think can go over to Walter Ephron on Monday. He's been looking for a horse just like this gelding."

"Do what you think is best," I replied. He'd bring the horses home anyway.

"How are the Zucks?"

"Both pinned in the flat class. It's raining hard and chilly so I'm going to try to bring them home after the fence class."

"How's the footing?" Lockie asked.

He always asked about the footing. I don't think he realized he was doing it, but he did.

"Not scary, but it's not draining as well as I'd like."

"It's coming down that hard?"

"It is."

"Tell them to trot the course if they're concerned."

"Okay."

"See you this evening," Lockie said.

"Be careful."

Lockie laughed. "I'm not driving."

"Then tell Dan."

"Tal."

"Put Wynne on the phone and I'll tell her to tell him."

"You're cute."

"And I have to go watch the fence class. Bye."

"Bye."

I turned and everyone had already left.

The rain was pelting down on the roof of the van almost like hail. It was going to be difficult to see if the deluge didn't let up soon.

I reached the warm-up area and motioned the girls over. "Lockie says to trot the course if you're concerned about the footing."

"How will we know?" Gincy asked.

"When you make your circle, make it tight. If it feels wrong, think about going slow. Beau will be perfectly happy to do that. Tango will be more keen, so you'll have to hang onto him a little, Poppy."

"I'm not worried."

No, Poppy was never worried. Gincy was the one who was always thinking about possibilities.

They were both smiling even though the rain was dripping off their visors. I wanted to kiss them they were so adorable.

The class was called and we all slogged our way to the ring, through the crowd of soggy equitation riders. The in-gate swung open and the first rider went into the ring, making a large circle to show her pony the fences. They all looked gray in the deluge.

We had gone over the course several times, but it was simple compared to what my girls did at home. This wouldn't be much of a challenge for them.

The little girl in the ring became confused at the third fence and took seven in the wrong direction. That was it for her.

Everyone who followed had some kind of issue but it all boiled down to the fact that the hard rain was distracting them. Some of the riders were dealing with slick tack, one girl was wearing glasses and couldn't possibly see, a few of them went off-course but a couple did very nice jobs.

Poppy entered the ring and made a tighter circle than anyone else. She didn't need to show Tango the fences since he was very reliable. The pony went into a canter and Poppy made it around the course perfectly.

We congratulated her showmanship and gave Tango well-deserved pats.

Gincy entered the ring, not quite as boldly and trotted a circle. I had no doubt whatsoever that whether she chose to trot or to canter, Beau would take good care of her. She put him into a canter, which, for Beau, was only slightly faster than a trot, and headed for the first fence.

"Are you holding your breath?" Greer asked me, as Gincy went down the diagonal.

"No. She's fine. We've practiced. These girls are tough, a little rain won't bother them."

Five jumps later, Beau was happy to be reined back to a trot and jogged out of the ring to be greeted by praise and pats as well as a small cookie from Mrs. Hamblett.

"Is there anything I could have done better?" Gincy asked.

"Not at all," I replied.

"The pace was too slow."

"Not for the conditions. You made a decision about what was right for you. That shows a lot of maturity."

Gincy smiled broadly and patted Beau's neck.

"Go take a walk around the grounds. Don't cross paths with the big horses, and come back here for the pinning."

They walked away, looking bedraggled but cute.

"Is there any reason to stay for the afternoon session," Aly asked.

"It's up to you and the girls."

"There's no chance either of them could win the championship?" Aly asked. "I wouldn't want to take that away from them.

"I suppose there's always a chance, but Tango was too expressive in the fence class and Beau was too slow." I replied.

"No. Robert Easton is here and in the other rings they're winning all the equitation classes," Greer said. "This is the only thing they concentrate on over there."

"We know." Mrs. Hamblett nodded.

"He's getting them ready for Fence Post Farm next month. It'll be the last big show of the summer so he wants to make an impression."

"Are we going there?" Aly asked.

"There's a cub hunt that morning and I thought the girls would enjoy being a part of introducing the young hounds to the process, but I'm not opposed to going to the show," I replied.

If it was experience we were seeking and fun, the cub hunt would be a better use of the day. There was another show at the end of the month that would be less competitive. They were still young and didn't need to be introduced to the finances of the rated horse shows yet. The Hambletts, and Aly, gave the girls everything they could, but there was also a budget we had to live with. The entry fees at upper level shows were as much as a car payment. That was reality.

"Look who it is," Cap said, motioning to the ring.

Ami Gish entered on Oneco. He was a gorgeous pony, with perfect braids and she was wearing a dry jacket. That was nice, having a spare. Most kids I knew couldn't afford that. I'd had one for the first few years I was showing. Then we had a summer weight and a spring and fall weight. In the winter, I wore insulated underwear.

She picked up a trot and started a huge, unnecessary circle. While Ami was dressed sharply, her position was no better than when she was riding at Bittersweet. If she could change one thing, turning her knee into the saddle would have made me happier. That one fault was pulling her whole leg out of alignment, making her less secure in the saddle.

Oneco was the ideal hunter pony, skimming over the ground, barely bending his knees except to jump.

"He's not going much faster than Beau," Greer said.

That was true. Oneco was not traveling at anything close to what could be called a hunting pace, but he was doing it with sophistication.

"He's not tracking straight," Greer said.

"She's not steering him," Cap replied.

Ami couldn't use her legs to keep him centered so she was over-compensating with her reins. One fence the pony would drift to the left, the next to the right, then she'd get lucky and they'd be in the center. Instead of settling in, the round was getting worse.

Everyone could hear Robert Easton coaching from the rail, which wasn't helping at all, but only confusing her.

"I don't want to watch," Cap said.

"Be strong," Greer replied.

There was a small gate fence and two strides to a small oxer. Ami made the turn for that line and it was like steering a car on glare ice. She managed to get Oneco over the gate but then had to haul his head around for the oxer.

In a state of complete disarray, the pony took a leap to make it over the fence and Ami flew out of the saddle in grand style.

19

"AIRBORNE," Cap commented.

Oneco trotted away, leaving Ami stretched out on the rails that had come down with her. She wasn't moving as the ringmaster and Robert Easton ran to the jump. Then came the paramedic. Then the ambulance and the gurney. The class came to a halt as Ami was gently lifted into the back of the ambulance, and driven away.

"It's probably just a concussion," Greer said. "They'll keep her at the hospital overnight for observation. She'll have a headache and that will be the end of it."

I looked at her.

"Why assume Ami broke something? How many times have we been tossed onto a fence?"

"True, but this was a hard fall."

"From a pony. We were coming off horses and it was a lot farther to go."

"I hope you're right."

The class resumed but all the remaining riders seemed shaken by the dramatic flying dismount. The judge and ringmaster pinned the class with Robert Easton's other two riders coming in first and second and Poppy and Gincy coming in third and fourth. They were satisfied but had had enough of being soaked and agreed it was time to go home.

After loading the ponies into the van, we bid the showgrounds a farewell as it started pouring again.

***

"I thought you were supposed to be gone all day," Jules said as we entered the kitchen seeking warm food and dry clothes.

"The girls were pinned in two classes. They learned what they went to learn and no one wanted to be wet for the rest of the day."

"I'll make some soup. How would you like cannellini bean and spinach?"

"I'd love it," I replied.

Jules went to the pantry and returned with our large pressure cooker. "Go up and change. If you're slow enough, lunch will be ready when you return."

I kissed her cheek. "Thank you."

We went up the stairs, and into our bedrooms. I stripped off the damp clothes, showered, then put on something soft and dry that hadn't found its way over to the carriage house yet. I was putting on some old shoes when Greer entered and sat on my bed.

"That pony was drugged, you know that, right?"

"I assume so. He was essentially drunk," I said. "Ami wasn't helping—"

"She was making it worse. Easton knows how much to give his horses to take the edge off. Maybe someone else dosed the pony."

"He had to know how incompetent a rider she is."

"Why would he know that?" Greer asked. "He may have had an assistant working with her and never really saw her until today. It's only been a couple weeks."

I thought for a moment. "What are we going to do?"

"If you mean about Easton, nothing. Even if we had proof, so what? He's doing what so many trainers do."

"Can Bittersweet Farm compete?"

Greer shook her head. "No. Not at the upper levels. Lockie and Cam with jumpers, yes. You know this is true."

"I do. Poppy and Gincy like the program as it is. If I take on new kids, they'll want to show. I don't want to have kids trying as hard as they can with no chance of winning."

"Like me and Nicole?"

"Yes. I wanted to see you get a championship over her once. I wanted you to throw your arms around Sans' s neck and be happy."

"You wanted that?"

"Selfishly." I smiled. "I hoped you'd be in a better mood if you won."

"Looking back, there were very few moments I enjoyed."

"I can say that, too."

"But, it's better now. A different life."

"Definitely. So what do we do? How do we do everything?"

"Define everything."

"You're running the Ambassador of Cheer, so for the time being, you're out of it. Lockie misses eventing."

"He's said that?"

"He's circled it without admitting it flat out. I thought Buck would satisfy the need to continue being a part of it, but he's gone."

"It's not a loss. That kid was always on the verge of doing something regrettable. Kitty?"

"She's temporary. I'm sure it'll help. He needs a dressage horse."

"What's wrong with CB?"

"They're having a personality conflict. I think it'll be worked out, but not immediately."

"Henry?"

I shook my head.

"We'll find him something."

"Splashie," I said.

Greer looked at me. "Did you hit your head, too?"

"Your mother's horse. Two-Tone."

"Roll the Dice?"

"I couldn't think of his name. I was watching him at Miry Brook. He has a lovely stride."

"He's a pinto."

"Technically, he's a skewbald."

"When's the last time we saw one of those in the dressage ring?"

"Not here, but in Germany."

"Is it a German horse?" Greer asked. "I thought it was an Appendix Quarter Horse or something and Greg got him off the track in New Mexico."

"I don't think so."

We headed down the stairs.

"He's my mother's hunter. Now that she's riding, I don't see how she'll give it up."

"She could ride Kyff. He likes women. Victoria's a woman."

Entering the kitchen, we saw bread, cheese and sliced chicken on the table. Jules was at the stove with a ladle in her hand.

"I suppose we're too late to help," I said.

"This was easy, but thank you for the offer. You could get your drinks. How about some music?"

"Where's Dad? Where Gram?" Greer crossed to the kettle.

"Your father went to meeting of like-minded individuals in Hartford with your grandfather, and your grandmother is visiting friends in Redding. We are alone."

I sat. "Do you want to go over to Rowe House Farm with us?"

"What?" Greer asked. "Why do we need to go there?"

Jules placed bowls of soup on the table, then took her seat next to me. "By choice?"

"Tal has a crazy idea of switching Victoria's hunter for Kyff so that Lockie can ride the neon horse in upper level dressage competitions."

Jules tried, unsuccessfully, not to laugh.

"It makes sense," I protested, reaching for some chicken.

"She has brain fever," Greer said.

"Since I know next to nothing about horses, why is this a crazy idea?" Jules asked.

"Because he's vulgar," Greer replied.

"He's not. And he's not responsible for his coat colors."

Greer gave me a look then turned her attention to Jules. "This is how it goes. We, British, created the style—"

"You're an American," I interjected.

"The upper class, the royals, my people—"

"They're your people when you need them, the rest of the time you have no respect for them," I said.

"Set the tone of how you were supposed to appear while riding. No bling, no bright colors to grab attention. Everything is supposed to be subdued, modest—"

I nearly choked on my cheese cracker. "If that doesn't describe Victoria, I don't know what does."

"It's common to be loud."

"The horse is loud?" Jules asked.

"Bays. That's what was the gold standard. For years even gray was a color nearly bred out of Thoroughbreds."

"Isn't that a bit extreme," Jules asked.

I nodded. "The British ride piebalds and skewbalds all the time so you'd better find another argument against Splashie."

"On the hunt field or for children. You don't see them in the dressage arena. When is the last time you saw a pinto in the Olympics?" Greer asked.

I thought.

"Right. Never. Why put Lockie on a horse with a color guaranteed to encourage disdain?"

"Because the horse is in the family and it could solve the problem now. Temporarily, at least."

Greer sighed. "Tch. The less we have to do with her, the better."

"I understand but it's for Lockie."

"Call her," Greer replied.

∞ 20 ∞

PICKING UP MY PHONE, I pressed in Victoria's number and waited.

"Hello."

"Hi, Victoria, this is Talia. How are you?"

"I'm fine. You wouldn't call unless you wanted something, so cut to the chase. What do you want?"

"Your horse. Roll the Dice."

"Why?"

"Because Lockie needs a dressage horse and after seeing you ride at Miry Brook, I think Dice would be good for him."

"Hunting season is starting soon, and that's my hunter."

"We'll trade you Dice for Kyff. It's just a temporary trial. I think Kyff would suit you well. There's a cub hunt coming up and you can see if he has the right disposition for your needs."

Victoria thought for a moment.

"We'll bring him to you."

"I'll bring Dice there. We can ride in the indoor and see if we're compatible."

"Fine."

Jules nudged me and whispered "Tea."

"We'll have a proper tea after," I said.

"You know how to make a deal, Talia," Victoria replied. "See you in a while."

"Thank you, Victoria." I put the phone down on the table.

Greer picked up Joly. "You will owe her until the stars fall out of the sky."

Jules pushed back from the table. "I have a lot of baking to do."

"I'm sorry for your extra work."

She leaned over and kissed me. "My pleasure."

***

About an hour later, Greg and Victoria got out of the truck and we helped him get Dice out of the trailer. The horse was bigger and showier than I remembered, but he had a kind eye and didn't drag me into the barn.

159

As I tacked Dice, I told Victoria about Kyff's background, and what his training had been. I made sure to tell her that Poppy had ridden him with no problems and expected him to be a gentleman on the hunt field. Which I believed to be true, at least after a few meets. I thought Victoria was a good enough rider to handle him if Kyff turned keen as everyone began to gallop. Under normal circumstances, I would suggest a double bridle for the first few outings but Kyff would probably be quite offended and over-react.

I got on Dice from the mounting block and walked with Greg to the indoor.

"Have you been doing any dressage with him?"

"I'm little more than a cowboy. He knows more than I do," Greg admitted. "I got him from a woman in Virginia who brought him over from Germany. He's a Hessen. No, it's not a well-known breed here, but there it is. She was spending her then-husband's money, so could afford to pay whatever it took. Then when they got divorced, she wanted to hit her ex in the pocketbook and forced him to take a huge loss on the horse. I thought Dice could be a jumper, but my life fell apart, so then it occurred to me he might be good for Lockie. Maybe he still will be."

"Maybe. How's he doing with Victoria?"

"This horse likes everything."

"Why doesn't Victoria sell him?"

"What does she need the money for? He's her field hunter. He's safe, the hounds can run under him and he can jump anything. They're good together. I hope that whatever you send us works for her."

"I'm sure Kyff will be fine."

"Victoria's been good to me. I haven't led a flawless life, but she hasn't held that against me."

"I'm glad to hear you're happy there. Are you happy there?"

"Yes. Someday I'd like to have my own place again, but right now, stepping away was the best thing to do."

Victoria entered the ring on Kyff and he wasn't doing fancy dance moves so he must have found her acceptable.

I had to give Dice a good squeeze to get him to trot, and it took me half way around the ring to adjust to his incredibly long stride. Being an international jumper was probably not in his near future. The way he covered ground, I thought he would have a difficult time in a speed class. Not that the speed was a problem, but the tight turns could be.

After warming up, I began to ask for the basics. Could he collect himself, engage his hind end, extend when asked?

Yes, yes, yes.

We did a shoulder-in and a half pass. He knew the drill but the movements were not yet refined or he'd lost his polish since coming from Germany.

I pulled up and he was perfectly happy to stand there while Victoria tried Kyff.

I was so proud of the progress he'd made since Florida. Time off then restarting had been just what Kyff needed. That, and the fact that we allowed all the horses to express their own unique personalities. They set the schedule and the training program. We just tried to guide them through the process.

As expected, Victoria had no trouble with Kyff and got him over the few jumps we had in the ring. In a way, he was a better size for her since she was about the same height as Greer, and Kyff was a couple inches shorter than Dice and not as round in the barrel.

She pulled up alongside me. "I'm willing to give it a try because Lockie needs a horse. I like Dice. We get along."

"I understand. It's just a trial," I repeated.

There was no way to know if Lockie would like Dice until he rode him. I didn't have enough knowledge to appreciate the potential drawbacks to his future as a dressage horse.

I didn't want Lockie to feel frustrated with his lack of progress and have that conveyed to CB. If there was no pressure, then CB would go along more happily. At least, that's how I had explained it to myself.

"We'll keep in touch," Victoria said as she dismounted.

"Of course, and if you want Dice back, no hard feelings."

Victoria looked skeptical.

I slid off Dice. "You're doing me a favor and I appreciate it either way."

We took care of the horses, then I walked Kyff into the trailer. "It's a vacation. You will have practically nothing to do over there and I'll come check on you. If you want to come home, just tell me," I said to him. "Just don't be stupid." I gave him a cookie and a pat.

Greg lifted the ramp and a moment later was driving toward Rowe House.

Victoria and I drove to the house while Greer went off in her wellies and raincoat with Joly.

"How is she?" Victoria asked.

"She's not the woman she senses she could be," I said.

"Is that my fault?"

"No. The Ambassador of Cheer project is doing well and expanding slowly. The Miry Brook show was very successful and raised quite a bit of money. She's gotten a couple calls asking if she would organize a show for other organizations."

"Charity work. That's not my side of the family," Victoria said.

"You could start small."

"Doing?"

I thought as we approached the house. "You have a big barn and lots of pasture. There are horses who need second careers. Greg is a smart barn manager and would get the horse in condition. In six months or a year, someone would love the horse to pieces."

"Interesting."

"Not bad publicity either." I opened the door for her.

"That would hardly be a consideration."

"Of course not."

"But I still have Rowe on Main. Equestrian antiques are always in demand." Victoria removed her jacket.

"Greer must have inherited her marketing skills from you," I replied.

"That wouldn't be a bad thing."

"She's helping a lot of people," I replied.

Victoria smiled.

Jules welcomed us in and we both went to wash up before sitting down at the table. By the time I had returned, Cap had arrived and a couple minutes later, Greer and a wet Joly.

We had steaming hot tea and delectable coconut honey cakes, garnished with strawberry fans. The discussion was about the show and Ami flopping off into the jump.

"It sounds as though she's not confident," Jules said.

"She has no reason to be other than people telling her she's wonderful," Greer replied.

"Gincy isn't as brave as Poppy but she knows her limitations," Cap said.

"I hate to see these girls riding horses they can't handle and competing in classes more advanced than they are." I finished my tea, thought about having a second cup then decided against it because CB was waiting for me whether he knew it or not.

"Greer went hunting with me when she was four," Victoria said.

Greer nodded.

"The pony was on a lead-line, of course, and we didn't jump, but we kept up. She was a natural."

"Maybe that explains how she was able to acquire sidesaddle skills so quickly," I replied.

"She was brilliant at Miry Brook," Victoria admitted. "Beautiful habit, too."

"She designed that," I said.

Victoria looked at Greer. "You're very talented. We haven't had an artist in the family for five hundred years, so it must come from the Swope side."

I pushed back from the table. "Unfortunately, I can't draw a straight line."

"As long as you can scrawl a course well enough that we can follow it, that's all you need to be able to do," Cap said picking up her plate and bringing it to the sink.

"We have chores," I said. "You're welcome to stay for dinner, Victoria."

Greer shot me a glance.

"If I'm not imposing—"

"It's no trouble at all," Jules replied.

"May I ask a favor?"

Greer groaned.

Victoria pretended to ignore the non-verbal commentary. "May I borrow a car? I told Teche I would visit him this afternoon."

"Of course. Take the farm car," I replied. "Otherwise all we have are trucks."

Victoria smiled. "Somehow I always pictured Greer driving country roads in a Jaguar XK-E."

"If it can't pull a trailer, it's useless to me," Greer replied.

I had to agree with her on that.

***

Later in the afternoon, Lockie was home with his equine acquisitions and I followed him into the lower barn. "What's this horse doing here?" he asked leading one of the new horses to a stall.

21

"DO YOU WANT THE LONG VERSION or the short?" I asked.

"The short."

"That's your new dressage horse." I opened the empty stall door for him and he walked the horse in.

"Maybe I should have asked for the longer version."

"I saw Dice at Miry Brook and thought he had potential. CB isn't cooperating, so maybe Dice will be something you can—"

Lockie removed the gelding's halter and left the stall without saying anything.

"I know his color is...atypical, but I was on him this afternoon and he knows quite a bit. I think you'll be surprised."

"Why would you get me a horse?"

"I know you miss eventing and thought if you had a horse you didn't have to struggle with so much, then—"

He put his arms around me. "That's very thoughtful of you and I will not look a gift horse in the mouth. How did you get Victoria to part with him?"

"I gave her Kyff."

Lockie took a deep breath.

"It's temporary. Just a trial," I replied quickly. "She rode Kyff this afternoon and thought he was okay. Greg brought him to Rowe House a couple hours ago."

"Is there anything you didn't think of?"

"I wouldn't know if there was, would I?"

We made sure all the horses were set for the evening, then went to the carriage house to change for dinner. The Ruhlmanns had gone to the inn so they could eat and get to sleep in order to head back to Kentucky early in the morning.

I wished they had been able to stay longer but it was in the middle of the summer when there were horses to train, students to teach, and events to attend. Maybe we could find some time this winter to go there for a visit. They had done so much for Lockie over the years, I really wanted to get to know them better.

We were the last to arrive at the house where everyone was already seated at the table including my father and grandparents. I knew something was wrong immediately.

"As everyone is aware, Dad and I went to a meeting today in Hartford with the campaign directors. I don't want to ruin your dinners but it's best if we get this out of the way," my father said, opening a large envelope and removing several photos. He passed them around.

Victoria glanced down then glared at him. "How could you let this happen, Andrew?"

"How do you suggest I could have stopped it? The photos were taken from the road with a huge telephoto lens."

The photo was handed from Jules to me.

It was a shot of Lockie and me leaving the carriage house early in the morning. I understood immediately, but wanted my father to say the words.

"Yes, these are photos taken by operatives to use against me in the election. My opponent will say my young unmarried daughter is cohabitating with the older man, her trainer. It will be made as unsavory as possible."

"This is my fault," Lockie said.

I felt sick to my stomach. "No, it's mine. I—"

"I should have been more responsible. I'll do whatever is necessary."

"Nothing is necessary!" Greer shouted from the other side of the table.

"I can leave," Lockie offered. "I should pack."

"No!" I protested. "I'll move back to the house."

"The damage is done," Jules said. "The photos aren't going away. Trust me. I've been through these manufactured publicity scandals before."

"I just wanted to be with him," I said.

"Everyone here knows you two should be together. Stop apologizing," Greer said.

Lockie turned to me. "We have to do what's right for your father. This is important to his life and–"

"Your relationship has nothing to do with his election," Victoria countered, hotly.

"It does," my grandmother said. "It brings his judgment into question.

"How?" I asked. "I don't drink. I don't do drugs. I don't anything. I work from sunrise to sunset. How does this reflect poorly on my father?"

"Because you just turned eighteen," my grandmother replied. "You didn't even graduate from high school."

I sat back. "Wait. Do you agree that it was poor judgment to allow me to live with Lockie? I'm an adult."

"On your father's property. With someone who works for him. Who knows when the affair began—"

"It's not an affair!" Greer interrupted.

My grandmother managed to ignore her. "It could have been last year when you were still a minor. I wouldn't have let it happen so easily, Talia. I think you're very young for a serious relationship."

"She wanted to be with him," Victoria responded. "Andrew missed out being with her mother. He didn't want to stand in Talia's way to enjoying whatever happiness she could have. We discussed this for days. It wasn't easy at all."

"Andrew and I discussed it," Lockie said. "I made him certain assurances and have kept those."

I felt like crying and when Jules took my hand in hers, my eyes filled with tears.

There was silence around the table.

"They know about Greer, too," my father said calmly.

Reacting in a flash of anger, Greer threw her plate against the wall. "So I'm screwed up! What does that have to do with you?"

"Wow. What am I missing," Cam asked as he stepped through the doorway, just missing the flying dinnerware.

171

22

JOLY BEGAN RUNNING back and forth barking.

"The Swopes in action!" Greer shouted, angrily, over Joly which only made him bark more excitedly.

"It seemed like the Coopers in action," Cam replied, taking off his raincoat and hanging it up.

Cam came over to me, leaned over, and whispered in my ear. "It'll be okay." He kissed my cheek lightly.

"You don't even know what's wrong," I replied.

"Nothing lasts." He grinned. "You saved a seat for me! Thanks!" He sat next to Greer. "Food or more drama first?"

Greer stood and was about to leave. Cam took her hand and wouldn't let her go. She sat back down.

"Let's all try to keep calm," my father said.

"Why do you imagine now is the time to be reasonable?" Greer demanded. "Our privacy has been breached!"

"The information hasn't gone public yet. It wouldn't do the opposition any good. If I should decide to run, that's when the mudslinging will start," he replied.

"Would anyone like to clue me in?" Cam asked.

Greer shoved a photo at him.

"Tal and Lockie leaving their house? What's so shocking about that?"

"It was taken from the road! Someone was hiding in the bushes waiting for my sister to leave the house with her boyfriend," Greer replied.

"And?" Cam asked.

"Make her seem like a slut," Greer said. "I didn't mean it like that, Tal."

I nodded.

"No one's going to care," Cam replied. "If she was leaving an opium den maybe that would make the news."

"They're going to say my father doesn't have any control over his children."

"Which is true since you're both adults."

"Cam, my indiscretions were not as an adult."

"No, as an adult, your behavior has been impeccable. Your temper, not so much."

"How can you laugh about this?"

I sank back into my chair. They were going to have one of their discussions that sounded very much like war.

"Whatever Talia has done, whatever you've done, has been exceeded by the behavior of families of most of the voting public. I'm sure this will not even register. They want to know what your father will do for them personally and whether or not his political outlook syncs with theirs. This is a lame effort by the other side to get him to quit."

Jules stood. "And on that fine point, I think it's time for dinner."

Even though the food was up to the high standards Jules regularly attained, I had no appetite. I just wanted to go home to where it was safe, until a moment after the thought, I realized that it wasn't safe and for all I knew someone could be spying on us again. Didn't they need a photo of us going in, too?

I wasn't sure what that proved, going in and coming out. I could have been at the big house and went in after dinner to play cards for a while. As for the morning photo, it was time-stamped, but how could they prove I hadn't arrived fifteen minutes before?

It wasn't about logic, it was about innuendo. The point was to make the public doubt my father's morality.

They had to know about my mother, too. That I had been born before my parents were married. That my father had been with my mother before his divorce to Victoria had been finalized.

Adding all these incidents together didn't paint a very pretty picture. I wasn't sure why none of this had occurred to me before this evening, but my mother had been the one interested in politics and not me. She would have been so upset by this, always believing that my father was an unusually ethical man.

All I wanted to do was take a shower so I could cry in peace for five minutes.

Greer stood. "Come help me walk Joly, Tal."

I nodded, left the table and dressed for the excursion into the rain.

We stayed to the driveway and Joly ran ahead of us.

"So all those years, you were so well-behaved and now your reputation is as tarnished as mine."

"That's not true."

"You're still better than me?"

"You deserve such a slap for that."

"Everyone makes mistakes. You made mistakes. I made mistakes. We have grown from those experiences." I paused. "The snapshot of a moment in time doesn't reveal the fullness of character. It's unfair what they're doing to Dad."

"Yes, it is."

"His first instinct is to protect us."

"And we want to protect him," Greer said.

"The choices we've made don't have anything to do with him. This is like extortion. The bad guys have information and if he doesn't do what they want—"

"Drop out," Greer supplied.

"Exactly. Then they go public. It's about forcing him to behave in a certain way. I think Cam's right and very few people will care. The person who will care—"

"Is Dad."

"Yes. And he must not give in to them. My mother would have been furious if he did. He must make this decision based on what's good for him, not to protect us from temporary embarrassment."

"Will you be embarrassed?"

"Very few people seek disapproval."

"I used to make bad choices but now I don't make any choices so I won't make bad ones."

I laughed.

"What should I do about Cam?"

"I told you. Walk up to him and take his hand. It doesn't have to be more than that."

"I'm not..." Greer paused, "pleased, with everything I did. If he finds out—"

"I see the dilemma. Since he's led an exemplary life, he'll be shocked to discover that you did not. A life that included being taken advantage of quite a few times by men who had no respect for you."

"Yes."

"It's Cam, Greer. You need to trust him."

"I don't know if I can."

"Okay. How long do you need before you can?"

"Is there a time limit here?"

"The horse world is full of girls looking for a handsome, straight guy with blond hair. You know that."

"Why would he be interested in me?"

"He says you're fierce."

"He said that?"

"Yes."

"He didn't say I was beautiful?"

"Yes, he's said that, too."

"More than once?"

I laughed and looped my arm through hers. "You have to do the rest of this yourself."

We arrived at the terrace and found Lockie and Cam leaving the house.

"We're going to your house," Cam said. "Have a couple beers and play some cards. Would you like to join us?"

"You're going to play cards now?" Greer demanded. "This is a crisis situation!"

I gave her arm a tug.

"If you don't think you have a prayer in hell in beating me at poker, that's fine. I'll see you tomorrow." Cam began walking away.

"Excuse me?"

"Did you burp? You're excused," Cam replied.

It was taking all my control to not burst into laughter.

"I can beat anyone at cards. Tell him, Tal."

"She's very proficient, Cam."

"Why can't we play here?" Greer asked.

"Because the adults are having a conversation," Lockie replied.

"What's wrong with my house?"

"Someone could be spying on us from the road," Greer said.

I thought for a moment. "That's true. We'll go look."

"I'll check," Cam said.

"Why you?" Greer began walking toward the driveway.

"Because I'm bigger than you and if someone needs to be punched in the nose, I'll do a better job of it. At least I'll be able to reach his nose. Come on, Lockie. Let's have a look."

They strode away leaving us on the walk.

"Why can't I just be nice to him?"

"You're scared to death of him, Greer."

"Why?"

"Because you don't want to be hurt. If you give up your anger, how will you protect yourself?"

"Didn't you worry about being hurt?"

"I worry about not experiencing the people in my life before they're gone."

"I'm sorry."

"No, my mother taught me a good lesson."

We walked to the carriage house and waited.

"My mother has taught me nothing of value," Greer said into the night.

"I'll bet that's not true. I'm not the expert gambler that you are, but it's—"

"All clear," Lockie reported.

"Did you see any tire tracks?" Greer asked.

"They got what they wanted," Cam said. "They took up residence rent-free in your head."

"How do we evict them," I asked as we went up the steps.

"They can't hurt you if it doesn't matter to you."

"It does matter. We have personal and professional reputations to consider," I replied.

"Those who know you, know the truth," Lockie countered. "No one else matters."

Cam pulled off his coat. "In my family, there is an expectation that the world must love you. That's what keeps actors both working and on the treadmill. Once people stop liking you, you stop working. I learned very early on that was not a life I could lead. People look to find fault because that elevates their self-worth. If you please them, their fragile egos would be damaged."

I removed my boots, took two steps toward the kitchen and stopped. "What is appropriate to offer with beer?"

"Snack food," Greer replied.

"Chips or...we don't have things like that." I tried to follow the lead Jules set—high nutrition, natural foods.

"Do we still have that summer ale or did you give it all to CB," Lockie asked.

I opened the refrigerator and took out two bottles of ale and two of sparkling fruit juice.

"That's perfect." Cam sat at the table and Lockie put the cards in front of him.

Greer sat across from Cam and he handed her the cards.

"She's a card shark," I warned him.

"So am I. What else do you have to do between scenes when you're eight years old but learn how to play poker from the crew?

We started to play and I was completely outclassed. After a few games, I gave up and went upstairs to read.

About an hour later, Lockie entered the bedroom. "They're professionals and they have something to work out between them."

"I hope it doesn't involve crying and throwing things."

"They seem to be determined to get the better of each other with cards this time." Lockie pulled off his shirt and headed to the shower. "I told them to turn off the lights and lock up when they leave."

I read until he returned. "Do you want to watch some television? Maybe wrestling is on."

"I'm tired. It was a long day. You didn't even get a chance to tell me about the show."

He got into bed and shut off the light.

"It poured. Robert Easton was there, so it was the Nicole Boisvert Factor. Ami Gish was there, too. She took a bad fall off Oneco. Greer and I think he was drugged."

"He probably was, then. How's Ami?"

"They took her to the hospital. Lockie, she doesn't know how to ride. She can pose pretty well, though."

"You had a full day, too."

"Surprises. One bad one after another," I replied. "I don't know where this leaves my father."

Lockie snugged up closer and took my hand. "I'm sorry. I just wanted to be with you."

23

"THIS HORSE DOESN'T KNOW MUCH," Lockie said as he rode Dice around the indoor, trying to see just how far his dressage education went.

"Then he's not spoiled," I replied. "Okay, you'll be entering at a lower level than with CB but at least you won't be going sideways."

"It feels like he's saying to me 'yeah, whatever'."

I could see that Dice wasn't as responsive as CB or Wing, which was probably why Victoria liked him so much for hunting. That wasn't necessarily a bad thing. Dice was capable of jumping big fences and keeping up with the field so he had energy that could be channeled into dressage.

Dice was a good mover. If we dyed his coat all one color, it would be a much different presentation. Lockie was probably thinking he had all this training to do to end up with a two-tone horse in the kind of competition where that would be unusual coloring at best and held against him by some judges at worst.

"Think of him as publicity."

Lockie pulled up and looked at me.

"He's eye-catching—"

"Garish is another word."

"He's brown and white. How garish is that?"

"Very."

Honestly, I was getting used to the splashes of color and Dice had a nice disposition.

"You'll stand out from the crowd. You're a fantastic trainer, a fantastic rider. Even if you don't win because of their biases, you'll get attention and we'll sell horses or training. I don't really see the downside."

"You don't."

"Someone may give you a great horse to ride. We don't know what possibilities may open up."

"That's true." He turned Dice back to the track. "What was the deal you made with Victoria?"

"That she could have use of Kyff or Keynote or whoever pleased her, and you could have Dice for a test period. Then we could discuss other arrangements."

Lockie pushed Dice into a trot and made a circle at the bottom of the ring. "He doesn't move away from my leg."

"I know."

Dice did, but not by a mere touch which was what Lockie expected in his dressage horse.

"He's out of practice. It's probably been two or more years since he was asked to do anything like that. The woman who brought him over from Germany was more rich than serious. She rode him when it fit into her schedule. Give the poor guy a chance."

Lockie went from the volte to a shoulder-in.

"Not bad."

Why I was on Dice's side was something of a mystery but I still thought he had potential. Nothing I saw in the next ten minutes convinced me otherwise. Considering that a Grand Prix dressage horse could cost a couple million bucks, Dice was a bargain. He just needed work.

Pulling up, Lockie came over to me. "I had a call from Kitty earlier."

"How is her mare?"

"They did the surgery but there's a long recovery so Kitty is sending her home when she can travel. That leaves her without a horse to ride this year."

"Yes?"

"Since Buck isn't coming back, what do you think of Kitty riding Wing?" He slid off Dice and ran up his irons.

I wasn't concerned that there were any sparks to rekindle on Lockie's side but wasn't sure about hers. He had meant something to her years ago, and the warm feelings remained so that he had stayed with her for several months after his accident.

Emotions could take on a life of their own. They flare up with unexpected fire, complicating relationships that were supposed to have entered another phase.

This was another step closer that Kitty would take to Lockie. If she was training on her own horse, she could leave at any time. If she was riding Wing, then there was a bond forming. She would always be in the middle of something. At least until the end of the season.

"He's your horse. This is your decision," I replied.

"Wing should be used for what he was trained to do. He's a good event horse."

"And Kitty needs a horse."

"At least temporarily until one can be found for her. I hoped this weekend trip would be more productive but either the horses were too young or—"

"They couldn't be too expensive," I said in disbelief.

"Old money doesn't behave in the same way as new money. She could spend whatever needed to get a made horse but that's not the way she was raised."

"So she needs your horse?"

"I wouldn't put it that way. He can move her along and do his job at the same time."

I didn't reply.

"What's your reluctance? Does it have anything to do with Kitty?"

"I think it's more about you."

"Me?"

We walked into the barn and I slipped Dice's halter on then removed the bridle.

"I would never part with Butch. I've collected ponies. No one but you and Greer has ridden CB since he's been here."

Lockie unbuckled the girth and removed his saddle.

"I brought Wing back for you thinking it would restore a part of your life that had been taken."

He leaned his saddle up against the wall and put his arms around me.

"When I came here, I had nothing. Now I have you."

I rested against him, feeling like a ship that had finally reached port.

❧ 24 ❧

"I'M GOING TO TAKE DICE over to Mauritz Schenker and get his opinion," Lockie said as we finished the morning chores. "Do you want to go?"

"I can't until later in the morning because I have a girl coming over to show me her pony. She wants lessons."

"Really?"

"She and her mom were at the deluge show and liked us."

"After that, are you free?"

"Sure, I'll take a ride to New York with you. Now you don't have to ask permission."

"The unexpected benefit of riding a horse who looks like a court jester in a harlequin costume."

"Lockie."

"All that's missing is the hat with the bells."

"You'll be sorry you mocked him," I said.

"I'm not. I'm teasing you."

"You can be sorry about that, too."

Lockie smiled. "Who's going to make me?"

The Zakarians' trailer pulled into the yard and stopped.

"Later." I walked past him.

"May I watch?"

"Watch or analyze?"

"We'll discuss. She'll be your student."

I nodded and went outside to see a young girl with short-cropped hair get out of the SUV.

25

"HI. I'M ANNIE."

"Hi. I'm Talia, and this is Lockie Malone."

Her eyes opened wide. "I've heard of you."

"Something good, I hope."

"I saw your photo in *The Gazetteer* on the winter circuit."

"That was me." He smiled.

Mrs. Zakarian came over, greeted us, and helped Annie get her bay pony out of the trailer. They quickly tacked him and Annie mounted.

"We'll go to the ring and you can just ride around for a bit," I said as we all walked over.

"Annie's been taking lessons for about two years and it's not that we expect her to be on the Olympic team, but her father and I feel that she's not making much progress."

"What makes you say that?" Lockie asked.

"Just trot around a few times and warm him up," I called to Annie.

Mrs. Zakarian watched her daughter for a moment. "I saw your riders at the show. They looked better than Annie does. Polished. With presence. As if they knew what they were supposed to do."

"That's very nice of you to say."

"I've watched Annie's lessons and they seem very similar from one week to the next. It's as if the trainer doesn't have much experience herself. She is a good rider," Mrs. Zakarian said.

"Not everyone can teach," I replied.

"That's exactly it. There are just so many ways you can say heels down before you need to step up to the next level. But that never happens and Annie always seems, to me, a little lost. This was her idea, so she must realize she's not getting much out of the lessons with her current teacher."

I nodded and went into the ring then motioned for Annie to come over to me.

"What's the last skill you acquired? I'd like to see it."

"We learned how to do a flying change."

"Brilliant! Show me."

Annie walked to the open area at the bottom of the ring while Lockie came over.

"What's she doing?"

"A flying change."

"I'm a little skeptical, but okay."

Annie began cantering her pony in a circle.

"This is not good," I said to him.

"Why not?"

"The pony's on the forehand and she's not sitting in the saddle."

They scrambled around in a circle, managed the lead change, and went to make the other half of the figure eight.

"Hold up there, Annie," I called.

She pulled to a walk.

"Can you sit in the saddle and lean your weight back just a little?"

I demonstrated from the ground.

She was baffled. "I don't know what you mean."

"You're in a modified two-point position." That's the term I used when Lockie called it the Pump and Bump. "Sit just like you were doing a sitting trot. Go ahead, try it now."

Annie went to the rail and began to canter, and had no clue how to sit.

"Sink into the saddle."

She didn't know how.

"Walk. Drop your stirrups and cross them in front of the saddle."

Annie did.

"Okay. Try it again."

She could barely stay on.

"Walk. You can cool him down." I turned to Lockie. "They're paying for lessons once a week and she can't ride without stirrups."

He shrugged. "Not everyone is as good as we are."

"What an ego."

"Factual. Should I get Dice ready for the trip?"

"Yes, but don't rush because I have to talk to the mother, don't I?"

"Are you going to take the kid on?"

"She's a nice girl."

"You just got rid of a girl, are you sure this one is easier to work with?"

"She seems to be."

Lockie went to the barn and I sat with Mrs. Zakarian at the picnic table explaining the Bittersweet Farm philosophy. I was willing to take students but we had to be compatible. If I was going to work hard for them, they had to work hard for me. I suggested they think about it overnight and see if they all agreed this was a good fit. There was a great deal of work to be done, but I felt confident Annie was capable. The question was whether or not she was willing.

Mrs. Zakarian thanked me and went to help Annie with the pony.

By the time I got into the barn, Dice was ready to go to New York for his debut. I unclipped him, held out a cookie and we walked to the van Lockie had driven into place.

Cap helped me load Dice, and asked if there was anything I wanted her to do while I was gone. I told her to take the Zucks on a trail ride and they'd have a lesson when I got back. I wasn't going to be gone but a few hours.

As I climbed into the cab, Lockie released the brake and we left the yard.

"If Mauritz doesn't like the horse, are you going to send him back to Victoria?"

"Probably." At the stop sign, he took the opportunity to glance toward me. "Why does that surprise you? I have a healthy ego, Tal, but I'm not under the delusion that I know everything. If the liabilities exceed the assets for this horse, it's not a profitable choice. We all have limited time, energy, and money. We should attempt to make wise and informed decisions about how we use our resources."

"If we don't know what's going to happen to us tomorrow, you should ride the horse you like today."

That was how the conversation went all the way over the state line into New York and until we parked at Balanced Rock Farm. I tacked Dice while Lockie changed into his good white breeches in the van.

"Try to make a good impression," I whispered to Dice and gave him a cookie.

Lockie came down the ramp.

He did have the perfect body for riding. Elegant. Long lines. There was a graceful way he carried himself naturally that few other riders possessed.

"What?"

26

"I'M SURPRISED you don't have a fan club."

"I do. A fan club of one and that's all I need."

"If you competed more often—"

Pushing his helmet onto his head, he led Dice to the portable mounting block. "I had all that when I was a junior." He got on and settled himself in the saddle. "I was hot in every sense of the word."

"Do you miss the attention?" I had a rag in my pocket, while wiping the dust from his boots, saw he was wearing spurs.

"When someone listens to you, fully, concentrating on what you're saying, not thinking about how they're going to answer or what they're going to do in ten minutes, that's the right kind of attention. The other stuff is static. It's never satisfying."

"I try. I'm not as good at it as my mother."

"I don't believe that for a minute. You're not trying, you do it. Now, let's see if Mr. Harlequin can work up some energy for long enough to please Mauritz."

After a brief warm-up in the outdoor arena, we met Mauritz in the indoor and there was already a small audience gathered. At least this time, I wouldn't have to hide under a blanket so I found a seat where I could both see and hear. Unfortunately, they were conversing in German and I could understand very few of the words. By the time I recognized a word, they had moved on past my translation abilities.

There were three young women sitting near me and I assumed they were working students. They watched with the kind of concentration serious riders would.

Lockie went out on the track and put Dice into a working trot. Dice was like a different horse. There was a crest to his neck, his ears were pricked forward, and he was engaging his hind end.

That was the difference between Lockie and me. He was a professional and I was someone who had just aged out.

As Lockie and Dice half-passed across the ring, the girls transformed into the Lockie Malone Fan Club. They loved him, they loved Dice, they wanted to know where he was from, and could he board at Balanced Rock.

Mauritz motioned Lockie to him and they had a discussion.

I loved that this was an intellectual process. Every movement was given consideration and thought through fully. What did the horse need? How could communication be improved with this horse?

With their own experiences in their history, Dice's personality wasn't similar to CB's. They couldn't be ridden, or trained, in the same way. The approach had to change with each horse and it was our responsibility to be flexible.

Of course, I never understood that before Lockie arrived. The deepest technical level Greer and I had reached was counting strides to a fence and making turns so that the judge would approve. That we learned that was remarkable.

At Long River one time, I had been walking the course with a girl who carried a digital distance measurement device.

"What's that?" I had asked, never having seen one.

"You point the laser at the jump and it tells you how many feet is between the fences. Carpenters and people like that use them. I don't know how to walk strides."

"Don't you ride with Jon Wainwright?" I was amazed. He produced more top junior riders than nearly anyone else. He wouldn't take us he was so exclusive, and so expensive.

"Yes, and he'd kill me if he saw this." She stuffed the gadget into the pocket of her hoodie. "I can't afford to switch trainers at this point and he hates me already."

I thought Lockie would be like our other trainers. The heads up heels down variety. It was quite a shock to find that he expected us to work. Quite often, I had wondered how, as a junior, he had managed to ride with people who were so much better than the supposedly top people who attempted to train us.

Maybe it was because there was money involved. A horse shown by Lockie would get publicity, ribbons, and a higher price tag. It was in everyone's interest to teach him as much as possible as quickly as possible because of potential sales. Our trainers just received a salary so there was no motivation to teach us anything beyond the basics.

Of course, Rui had been finding ways to enhance his income on the side from the beginning, we later learned.

Dice missed two lead changes coming through the diagonal but it was obvious that he had been well trained in Germany and when asked to perform, he turned out to be something of an egomaniac, all too happy to take center stage and wow the crowd.

Seeing Dice's comportment, made me hope Lockie was changing his opinion about the horse.

Maybe Dice realized he was never going to be lost in the crowd so he'd capitalize on his coloring and really show off. He was holding nothing back and even had a little toe flip to his extended trot making the girls next to me nearly swoon.

Lockie went back to talk with Mauritz, dismounted and ran up his stirrups. After glancing toward the viewing section, he saw me and motioned me over.

"Do you groom for him?" One girl asked.

"Yes," I replied.

"You're so lucky."

"I am."

Crossing the arena, I went to stand next to Lockie.

"Mauritz, you remember Talia Margolin, who owns that opinionated gray Hanoverian."

"Yes, the one with the sense of humor. Lockie tells me you encouraged him to ride this horse."

"I did."

"You were correct in doing so."

"That's kind of you to say. Lockie was concerned about his color. Do you think that will be a drawback?"

"In America? Perhaps," Mauritz replied. "In Europe? Years ago, I had a very talented Hessen who looked much like this one."

I wasn't sure if his then and our now could be compared. "Is it worth it to spend time on him?"

Mauritz regarded me with surprise. "He's a wonderful horse and will make an outstanding competitor. As for the coat of many colors, someone has to change minds. Let it be this boy." He gave Dice a firm pat on the neck.

I wondered what Lockie would say.

I wondered what Victoria would say.

Lockie handed me the reins. "Would you take care of him, while I take care of some business?"

"Sure."

Mauritz and Lockie walked away and I turned Dice toward the van.

"Thank you." I pulled a cookie out of my pocket and offered it to him.

He ate it then sneezed on me.

27

WE HAD A LATE LUNCH and I hurried back to the barn to give the Zuckerlumpens a lesson. It would be the first time Gincy would ride Oh Fudge. He wasn't the dressage pony she wanted, but he had a great deal to teach her about collection. Poppy would be on Calling All Comets who could teach everyone at the farm something.

I found Day on the aisle, brushing Moonie. "You're back from fishing. Did you catch anything?"

"Lots. It's a competitive sport for my grandmother. We didn't go to the store once. She's tougher than she looks."

"Impossible."

Sibby Jamieson looked tougher than a sumo wrestler.

"Poppy says they're having a lesson. May I ride in with them?"

"Sure, but why? Wouldn't you like to wait for Lockie?"

"You'll be covering the same exercises," Day replied.

"Yes."

"Some of the horses will be shorter than others." She laughed.

"It's okay with me."

"Cap asked me to tell you that you have three phone messages on the desk. Prospective students."

"For Lockie?"

"I understood they were kids who wanted to ride with you."

"Let me go have a look and I'll meet you in the ring."

In the tack room, there were three messages for me. Seven were for Lockie, five looking for horses, two wanting a new trainer.

Wondering what had changed and why people were suddenly contacting us, I went to the lower barn to check on the ponies and to find Greer. Cap was overseeing Poppy and Gincy who looked as if they had spent not the one day at the barn, but two. Predictably, Greer was in her office.

"Did you know we've been getting calls for horses?"

She handed me three pieces of paper. "The 4-H Club wants lessons, Mrs. Meade says the county fair has an emergency and needs a judge for the pie contest, and Annie Zakarian wants to ride with you."

"Go back to the pies."

"It's for Jules."

I nodded. "That makes sense. Why didn't she call the house?"

Greer didn't look up from her paperwork. "This was the number she had."

"You didn't say what happened with the poker game."

She put her pen on the desk. "He won. I won. He won. I won. At midnight, we gave up. I went home and he went home. Don't look at me like that."

"I'm not looking at you in a special way."

"You're looking sorry for me."

"I am sorry for you." I turned to leave.

"How did Dice do for Mauritz?"

"Spectacular."

"What?"

"Oh yeah."

"That clodhopper? That field hunter? My mother's babysitter?"

"Go figure. He likes everything—Lockie, cookies, work, standing, sleeping, galloping. He's a big show-off."

Greer was in disbelief.

"There were some working students there to watch. He made himself big, arched his neck, and did an extended trot nearly as good as CB's."

"No. You're having me on."

I shook my head.

"But the color disqualifies him from serious consideration."

"Not according to Mauritz."

Greer sighed. "What's my mother going to say when she wants this horse returned and Lockie is in the middle of training him for an important competition?"

"Kyff should make her a perfectly serviceable horse, or Keynote could."

"Does that sound like my mother?"

"She hasn't been that bad lately. Maybe she's growing up."

Greer screeched at me and I left to do my lesson.

By the time we were done, they were hot and tired and I was just hot. Jules came to the rescue with freshly made gelato.

"I've been experimenting," she said, holding out the cooler containing portions of ice cream, each with a small spoon.

The Zuckerlumpens reached for theirs enthusiastically and dug in.

Day and I took ours.

"It tastes like Good and Plenty candy," Gincy said making a face and putting hers back in the cooler. "I don't like licorice."

"It's fennel," Jules replied. "A vegetable in the carrot family. See the little leaves."

Scooping up a small spoonful, I put it in my mouth. I struggled to think of something positive to say. "How creative."

"You don't like it." Jules was disappointed.

"I do. I think it's delicious." Day licked her spoon.

"I'm just accustomed to...fruit or chocolate," I said. "Maybe I'd get used to this."

Jules took the cup of gelato from me. "That's not necessary."

"We're not sophisticates here. Maybe Greer is, but I'm just a farm girl."

Jules smiled. "My feelings aren't hurt. You don't have to dig the hole any deeper."

"Phew."

"There are fresh chocolate chip cookies at the house for the unadventurous types," Jules said.

"May we, Tal?" Poppy asked.

"As soon as you take care of the ponies."

"Their comfort always comes before ours," Gincy repeated what I had said to them many times.

"Good girl."

As we were walking into the barn, one of the bright red Acadiana pickup trucks drove in and parked.

Emma Crocker jumped out. "I just had a fight with Mill. May I stay here for a while?"

"Sure. Cap's inside getting ready to ride," I said. "Do you want to ride?"

"I'd love to. It's so boring over there. Most of their horses are here except for the polo ponies and Mill won't let me ride them."

"We got a new horse in earlier in the month, would you like to ride him?"

"Sure!"

"Cap's with the pony riders in the lower barn. Tell her you're riding Available, and she'll help you with him. You help her with Spare, and see if Greer wants to ride Tea."

I headed for the ring to move the jumps.

Fifteen minutes later, I was watching my crew trot around the ring. Everyone looked comfortable but the pair that surprised me was Emma and Available.

Cap had told me Emma was inclined to trail ride most of the time and it was just something she did for fun. That was not the picture I was seeing.

"Walk, please. Emma, have you been taking lessons?"

She slumped in the saddle. "It shows? At the Cadiz Day School you're required to take a sport. I looked on the list and everything involved chasing after a ball, except the horseback riding. So in order to avoid softball or field hockey, I've been learning how to ride all prim and proper."

"It's apparent you picked something up," I replied.

"I thought I could hide it," Emma said.

"Don't. It looks good."

"I'll go home, help Dad with the farm and ride Pichou through the orange groves like always. I don't have any use for being fancy."

"We might," I said. "With all the new horses coming through the barn, I could use one more jockey."

There was a limit to how many horses we could ride each day. It wasn't that we had as many horses as some barns, but we allocated our time differently. We trained lightly then took the horses into the hills. Sometimes that was for conditioning purposes, sometimes it was for relaxation, but it was an investment in time. One more rider would ease everyone's schedule.

"I don't know when I'm leaving. Mill's...being impossible. Staying with him is not the best way to spend my summer."

"Stay with me," Cap said. "I don't hold anything your brother did against you."

"Are you sure?"

Cap nodded. "We were friends first."

"In that case, maybe."

"Think it over." I gestured toward to the rails and jumps. "I have two gymnastics for you. One pony-size, one horse-size. If it were me, I would drop my stirrups but don't take that as a suggestion of what you should do."

Everyone in the ring was strong enough to ride the low fences without stirrups and they all crossed their irons in front of the saddles.

"I want you to stay close to the saddle. Sit on the way in, then let the natural motion help you stay with your horse."

Poppy nodded. She was always so serious.

"Are you feeling good on Call," I asked her.

"He's very nice."

"Jump the gymnastic."

Poppy trotted away, turned for the line, sat in the saddle and let Call carry her over the fences.

"Very nice!"

She cantered up to me. "Very nice for me or very nice in comparison with everyone?"

"I don't want to compare you to everyone but it could hardly have been done better."

"Really?"

"Yes."

"Yay."

"Gincy, you go."

For my little dressage enthusiast, Gincy also did a nearly flawless line and we all applauded.

The horse riders went and I was a bit more critical, asking for them to pay attention to where their legs were.

"Use your whole body to feel the horse. Knees against the saddle but not pinching. Sit in the saddle not on it. Nice, Greer."

Of course, Greer would be perfection.

Cap hadn't had the benefits of intense equitation training so she was still a little rougher around the edges. To some, it wouldn't make a difference now that she was an adult, but it mattered to Lockie, so it mattered to us. If a rider wasn't balanced in the saddle then the horse would have to compensate. Over the lower fences, it wouldn't be important, but over the bigger fences, it could mean a rail down or general disorganization, which could result in time faults, injury or a fall.

Lockie wanted us to strive for precision. We didn't have to be perfect, but we were expected to know the ideal, and why it was valuable.

We worked over the gymnastics until everyone was starting to get tired and then I suggested a ride to the stream for a drink of cool water.

"You, too?" Greer asked.

"I'll be right back."

I jogged to the barn, put a halter and lead rope on CB, brought him outside and got on from the mounting block.

Lockie came up from the lower barn at that moment and saw I didn't even have a bridle on CB. "You just do that to humiliate me."

"You could do this."

"And get all that gray hair all over me? I don't think so. See you later."

∽ 28 ∽

LATER TURNED OUT TO BE when afternoon chores had been completed and I found him on the lounge chair. Even though the heat of the day hadn't dissipated, I crushed in next to him.

He managed to get an arm around me. "You had to find a way to cover me with gray hair."

"I have nothing else in my life to worry about besides that."

"He likes you. Me not so much."

"Could be two things. He doesn't know you very well and probably men abused him, so he would remember that."

"I could say something clever about CB just being a horse, and they don't have the intellectual acuity to understand but look at Greer."

"She's paralyzed."

"You can't tell people to just get past it and then they do."

"No. It's a slow process but it happens," I replied. "Why, though?"

"I think it's the way our brains work."

"How so?"

"The logical functions are the least powerful. The self-preservation instinct is the oldest and most powerful. It's hard to override what you believe threatens you."

"How do we convince Greer that having a relationship with Cam won't destroy her?"

"Hang on. That's none of our business."

"Lockie."

"Talia. It's not."

"You're right."

"Thank you."

"I'm sure you would have found it much preferable to slog alone on your own without any help from me."

"Low!"

"Well..."

"It's not the same and you know it."

"It's my sister."

"You and I made a choice to go forward together. That's not a choice you can make for Greer and Cam."

"I'm trying to help her to become more comfortable, the same way we tried to make Kyff more comfortable with the nylon bit. It's not specifically about Cam."

"What do you suggest? I can say no at any time, I reserve that right."

"Okay. If they were in proximity more often, that would be good. Playing poker was good."

"Nothing came of it."

My phone began ringing and I reached for it. "It's a step," I said to him. "Hello."

"Hi, Tal. We're going out to dinner. Would you and Lockie like to join us?" Jules asked.

I looked at him. "Is Greer going?"

"Yes."

"May we invite Cam?"

Lockie gave me a hard squeeze.

"Certainly."

"Where are we going?"

"The Liondrake."

"What kind of word is that?"

"I don't know. Are you calling Cam or am I?"

I thought for a moment. "You, please. See you in a while."

"What kind of word is what?"

"Liondrake."

"Like a mash-up between a duck and a lion?"

Trying picture such a beast, I laughed. "Yeah. So instead of roaring, it quacks?"

"Did you accept a dinner invitation for me?"

"Yes, I'm sorry. Would you like to go or stay home?"

Lockie stood. "I don't really want to get dressed up but I'd like a steak."

***

Too bad, because an hour later we were in the newest restaurant in Reynolds Bridge, looking at little dabs of food artfully arranged on our plates.

"I want to stop at the Grill Girl on the way home and get dinner," Lockie said.

Cam pushed back from the table and held his hand out to Greer. "Let's go now."

"Guys, come on. This chef worked at The French Laundry."

Greer glanced at her plate. "That's the problem. He doesn't know how to cook, but maybe he knows how to remove stains."

Jules made a face. "The French Laundry is a very famous restaurant. One of the finest in the country."

"Okay," Cam replied as he placed his plate, then Greer's, in front of Jules. "Now that's a human portion. Thank you for inviting me, it was memorable."

"Go on. We'll see you later," she said.

We left my father and Jules to the photogenic food and made it to the Black Angus burgers smothered in caramelized onions and twice fried fries before we starved to death.

***

The horses were fed, the night shift came in, the morning shift went out and we went up to the house for breakfast. My father was sitting at the table, a bowl of fresh fruit in front of him and a cup of coffee in his hand "You left yesterday evening before I had a chance to tell you what the family's future looks like."

"I'm sorry." I dried my hands with a towel. "I thought it was just another ridiculous restaurant experience and we wouldn't be missed."

"It was a little *avant garde*, wasn't it?"

"The miniature octopus crossed the line for me," Lockie said.

"Baby," Greer corrected.

"Worse." Lockie sat at his place.

Jules brought the frittata, I brought the basket of freshly baked rolls to the table, and we sat.

"I've given this proposal my full concentration for the past two months. I've talked to my parents, lawyers, and political people whose judgment I trust. I've spoken with each of you and listened carefully. The decision is ultimately mine and mine alone."

"May I interrupt for a minute?"

"Greer," I said to her. "Let him finish."

Greer ignored me. "If you spoke with my mother, it's a guarantee she gave you bad advice. Whatever you decide, we'll make it work."

Under the table, I felt Jules' hand pat my leg.

"That's very generous of you, Greer. What do you want? Personally. For yourself." My father waited for her answer.

"That's been my whole life. It's always been about what I wanted. That's not something anyone should give credence to."

"Humor me. I would like to know," he said.

She took a moment. "I've been studying the political climate since this offer was made to you. I've read everything the Swope Foundation has printed in the past four years and it's easy to draw some conclusions. We can do more behind the scenes than in front. I'll work with you, and do whatever Tal's mother did. I want you home with us. It's selfish but that's what I want."

My father nodded. "I agree."

There was silence at the table.

"Excuse me. Did I understand that correctly?"

"I said no thank you to the committee," my father replied. "More can be done behind the scenes. My energies will be neutralized if I should get elected. It's not a given that I would win the race, but if I did, I don't know what I could accomplish. It's not the kind of job you should take if you don't have a passion for it."

"That's behind us." Greer reached for a morning bun.

***

As Lockie tacked Dice for his session, I finished buckling the last boot on the gelding's leg and stood. "I've been thinking about the girls who want to ride with me."

"You shouldn't think."

"Too late. How many hours did you ride a day when you were a junior?"

"Six or more. I rode every horse they could find for me. Sometimes I went to school. Sometimes I did a correspondence course. In the early years, I didn't have an Amanda to tutor me."

"How many lessons did you have a week?"

"I was being watched all the time."

"Exactly," I replied. "One lesson a week will make so little difference."

"That's not true. You'll give them homework. They'll maximize their time in the saddle by riding without stirrups. It can be done. They won't get to the Kentucky Horse Park but they'll learn and make progress."

"Should I assign reading material?"

"That's an excellent idea." Lockie led Dice out of the barn and to the mounting block. "Tal, don't go overboard on how responsible you can be to these kids. They're coming to you for a lesson, not to become a Medal finalist by next season." He mounted.

"I won't speak for Greer, but I learned a lot in the past four years. You're the only trainer who really did right by us. There were a couple who were honest and competent, but overall, three of those years were not a positive experience."

"Got it, but don't overcompensate. These riders are coming here without that background. You won't be a negative experience. That would be impossible. You'll bring them along and if they want to do more, they'll let you know."

We walked to the indoor because it was better for him to ride in the shade.

"I feel like I should send Ami Gish a get well card. Gincy says her leg will be in a cast for a couple months."

"Stay out of it." Lockie pulled up. "You're a professional now. When horses or riders leave, be like me, have amnesia. Don't think about them. Don't remember them."

"It's a gesture of kindness," I said.

"I understand, but no. Cut the ties."

I looked up at him. "If you left the farm, you would never talk to me again?"

"You're thinking. What did I say about that? I said don't. We're not in a business relationship. Besides, you said I could stay here forever, so you'd be the one leaving." He trotted off on Dice.

"This is my home. I'm not leaving."

"That could become awkward if we're both living here and you're not talking to me."

"I'm not talking about this anymore. It's too crazy."

"Perfect. How about if we talk about dressage? What do you think Dice's issues are and what's the one I should work on this morning?"

"Don't you know?" I asked.

"Now you're not just talking to me you're talking back."

"Enough. I was teasing but the truth is I really don't know."

"Tell me something about this horse." Lockie passed me doing a sitting trot.

"He has a great long stride."

Lockie made a small volte.

"He's a little disorganized. For a field hunter it wouldn't matter, but he needs to be pulled together a little. In a frame."

"Right. How are we going to do that?"

My mind searched for the answer. Everything. "Basics. Balance."

"That's what we can do. Instead of plunging around covering ground, we'll encourage him to hold himself together. The horse must carry himself. The rider should do as little as possible but as much as necessary."

"Fortunately, he's not green."

"Dice knows the material to a certain extent, but he's a bit rusty, so we'll go back and remind him. He needs to be responsive to the aids, keep his balance, and engage his hind end."

For the next twenty minutes, I watched Lockie ride Dice, explaining every movement, through the serpentines, circles, and diagonals. Dice dropped onto the bit and began to respond to the reins and Lockie's legs.

They walked.

"Can you come here, please?"

Lockie steered Dice and stopped alongside me.

"Bend down," I said.

Lockie leaned over and I kissed his cheek. "Don't not talk to me."

"I'm promise, Tal. I will not not talk to you."

"Am I interrupting?" Day asked. "Of course I am. You're kissing. Are you done kissing or are you going to continue?"

"We're done," Lockie replied. "Is there something we can help you with?"

"The hunt's going cubbing tomorrow," Day said.

"I know, we're all going."

"The whipper-in had one too many tipples last night, with the predictable results."

"He's out of commission," I said.

"Yes. We need a whip and most of the members are out of town on vacation."

"What's the matter with you?"

"If I could clone myself, yes, but I'm already the substitute whip."

"Can't Sibby come up with someone?"

"My grandmother is at home calling around, but every club's going out tomorrow."

"If you can't find anyone else, I'll do it," Lockie said.

"You?" Day asked.

"Is that so hard to believe?"

"Um...yes."

"I'm sure what she means is that you're riding in a dressage saddle right now and...I don't know what she means."

"When I lived in Ireland, I was the whipper-in for the Ballyna Blazers. It was only for a season but they seemed to think I wasn't half bad at it."

"That solves the problem then." Day smiled.

29

WE PULLED INTO THE JAMIESON FARM like the circus coming to town. There was our van, Cam's trailer, Lockie's trailer, Aly Beck's trailer and the Zakarian's trailer.

The sun wasn't up when Lockie woke and started to get ready. I lay there for a moment thinking it was just too early.

I had been at the house with Jules and Greer watching an old movie and testing all-natural gummy Olivers, which were delicious. Her creativity with food was constantly a delight, except for the fennel gelato.

We needed that time together to talk about everything that was going on at the farm. It had been non-stop activity since the party, and finally, things seemed to be returning to

221

normal. My grandparents had left for Prince Edward Island. Kitty had taken her mare back home and was staying there for a while to make sure she was settled in. Victoria hadn't complained about Kyff.

Mrs. Meade had called and asked Jules to judge the pie contest at the county fair next month. We had to talk her into that and she only agreed if we would sit there with her for the judging. Greer and I would be at the fairgrounds anyway because of the horse show. Poppy and Gincy weren't members of the 4-H but some of the new students were.

With all that talking and eating, by the time I had gotten to the carriage house, it was later than I had planned. After quickly showering, I got into bed and imagined Lockie as whipper-in, puppies running everywhere, pony riders running everywhere, and what could possibly go wrong with Victoria and Kyff. Too many variables for me.

I got out of bed. Time to go hunting.

We had just gotten Lockie on Dice when Day came over on Moonie to introduce him to the staff and he left with her.

Cap and I got Greer on Tea, then concentrated on Poppy, Gincy and Annie. As Greer returned to bring them to the group, Cam and Jetzt went past at an unnamed gait but since Cam was laughing, it must have been enjoyable. It was Jetzt's first hunt.

"Avoid him," I called to the Zuckerlumpens.

"It's like organizing the army," Cap commented as she and Emma went to get Spare and Available out of the trailer.

I went up the ramp and put my arms around CB's neck. He smelled good and I wondered if he thought the same about me or if the scent of cookies overrode every other consideration.

Ten minutes later, Cap, Emma, and I joined the hunt. The ponies were going with the hilltoppers, the flight for the green or older horses and riders who wanted to enjoy the day without getting in the way of the larger, faster horses. Greer and I had started out as hilltoppers years ago and since the group didn't follow the rest of the field, because it had to find its way around fences, often we had gotten a better view of the action.

We moved off at a walk toward the Jamiesons' fields, bordered by perfect stone walls. Poppy and Gincy waved at me. They were so happy.

Greer came up alongside me. "Lockie looks lovely."

He was on the right side of the pack keeping them together, while Day did the same on the other side.

"Yes, he does."

Behind us, a horse snorted. I didn't turn around to look. "Jetzt."

"He's gone on trail rides with us. I don't see why he has to be so upset."

"Maybe it's the hounds."

"I hope he doesn't step on one."

"We'll be disinvited," Greer replied.

A moment later, we were all cantering up the hill, and Jetzt passed us. I thought I might have heard Cam shout "Yahoo!" as he went by.

The country was beautiful and we went in a different direction than we had for the hunter pace the year before, so it was all new to us. The fences were sturdy but not particularly large, nothing our horses couldn't handle.

After trotting through the woods, we reached a field with a lake to one side. There we had a check. The hilltoppers weren't with us and I hoped they were having a good time. Both girls had phones on them, and knew to call me if there were any problems.

"Did you see your mother?" I asked.

"No."

I hadn't seen Victoria. "She loves hunting and said she would be here."

"How many times has she said she'd do something and then didn't?"

"True, but it seemed like she's gotten better."

"Don't fall for it."

The field began to move off again at speed. Word filtered back to us that someone had seen a coyote.

By the time, Sibby called it a day, no one had seen a coyote, fox or even a squirrel. We returned to the vehicles and began preparing to leave.

"This was the best morning!" Poppy exclaimed as she got off Tango.

"You had fun?" I asked.

"It was great. When do we get to ride with you?"

I had to think fast. "Some of the fences are bigger than Tango can handle."

"Maybe I could ride a horse. Keynote?"

Greer looked at me. "Yes, Tal. Maybe she could ride a horse."

We needed a small junior hunter. "We'll see."

"We get to do the hunter pace, right?" Gincy asked.

"Yes. There will be a low option or a go around."

"Yay!"

"Cheer later," Aly said. "Let's take care of the ponies now."

"I can do the hunter pace?" Annie asked.

"We'll talk about it," her mother replied and led her back to their trailer.

Emma came up, slid off Available, and gave him a big pat on the neck. "He was so good!

Cap dismounted from Spare. "He sure was. Nice horse.

After taking care of the horses, we loaded them onto the van. We would have been going down the road but Lockie and Cam were not in evidence.

"You can go," I said to Greer. She had driven Lockie's rig with Spare and Available.

"Are you sure?"

225

"You don't need to hang around when everyone else is leaving. I'm sure they'll turn up soon." I wasn't sure of that at all but it was good to say.

Aly Beck's rig was following the Zakarian's rig down the drive through the field.

"Okay. Then we can help you more easily when you get home."

Greer, Cap and Emma left.

I went up the ramp and sat on a bucket. "We've been abandoned."

CB pushed his nose at me and I gave each of them the last of the cookies.

"So spoiled. And you so deserve to be."

About ten minutes later, Lockie and Cam showed up.

"Talia? Are you still here or did you get a ride home?"

I came down the ramp. "You're my ride."

"See you at home," Cam said and rode to his trailer.

"Sibby wanted to talk to us."

"Did Cam and Jetzt pass her in the field?" That was a big mistake.

Lockie began untacking Dice. "No, she asked me if I'd be interested in helping out once in a while."

"Really. That's a surprise. What did you say?" I handed him the halter and took the saddle from him.

"If it doesn't conflict with a show, yes, I'd consider it. What do you think?"

"I think you looked beautiful."

"Tal. We're trying to be serious."

"Greer thought so, too."

He shook his head.

"You'd be very careful, though, right?"

He put his arm around me. "Extremely careful. Dice is a good field hunter. He went well and didn't step on more than two or three puppies."

"Lockie!"

"No point in bringing them back. Left them up in the woods so no one would know. Don't tell, okay?" He was teasing.

I bumped him with my hip. "You're so bad."

Lockie laughed as he led Dice up the ramp.

***

We got home, parked in front of the barn. I could feel that something was wrong when I saw Kate standing next to Cam.

"What happened?" I asked.

I felt Lockie reach for my hand.

"It's not that bad," Cam said. "No one is dead."

"Cameron!" Kate gave him a jab.

"We'll fight it," Greer assured me.

"Fight what?"

"Ami Gish's father is suing you for a half million dollars," Kate said. "Paul told me you'd be hearing from his lawyer."

I was speechless.

"What's he suing her for?" Lockie asked.

"Malpractice, irresponsibility. He claims Ami was injured at the show because of your teaching methods."

I still couldn't speak.

"Your system is so different than the rest of the world, that it caused her to become confused and have the accident."

"It's classic. It's the George Morris style!" Greer exclaimed.

"She was a student of Robert Easton's at the time," I managed to say.

"He's being sued, too," Kate replied.

"Why sue me?"

"Because your father has deep pockets and will do anything to make this go away," Cam explained.

"We'll fight. We're not giving in. This is extortion!" Greer said. "We'll countersue!"

"Everyone calm down," Lockie said.

"Does my father know?" I asked.

"Not yet."

"Lockie," I said to him. "I was just starting to get somewhere with Zuckerlumpens and this will destroy my reputation."

"That's the reaction Paul Gish wants," Greer replied. "That's why Dad will pay him to shut up. What a skel!"

Cam turned to Kate. "Yeah, Mom. Why are you his friend?"

228

"What do I have to do with this?"

"Don't blame her," I said.

"Stop!" Lockie said. "I know everyone is upset but, trust me, the emotion is wasted."

Up until that moment, I hadn't realized how much I had wanted to teach, to help young riders become horsewomen in the fullest sense of the word. It felt as though this was being taken from me.

I hadn't yet gotten past the phase in my life when it was defined by loss.

Lockie kissed my cheek. "We'll get through this," he whispered into my ear.

 The End

Join our mailing list and be among the first to know when the next Bittersweet Farm book is released.

Send your email address to:

barbaramorgenroth@gmail.com

Note: All email addresses are strictly confidential and used only to notify of new releases.

WHO'S WHO AT THE FARM

Talia Margolin—18 year old trainer at Bittersweet Farm, her horse is Freudigen Geist, stable name CB, Butch her junior horse and two ponies Garter and Foxy Loxy.

Greer Swope—Talia's 18-year old sister. Her horses are Counterpoint, Citabria (stable name Bria) and Tea Biscuit her junior hunter.

Andrew Swope—their father

Sarah Margolin—Talia's mother, now deceased, Andrew's ex-wife.

Victoria Rowe—Greer's mother, Andrew's ex-wife

Julietta "Jules" Finzi—private chef and confident to the girls.

Lockie Malone—head trainer at the farm, Talia's love interest. His horse is Wingspread.

Cameron Rafferty (Cooper)—show jumper, Greer's potential love interest. His horses are Whiskey Tango, Jetzt Oder Nie and his childhood pony, Remington.

Kate Rafferty Cooper—Cam's mother

Fitch Cooper—Cam's father

Kerwin Rafferty—Cam's grandfather

Caprice "Cap" Rydell—barn manager, her horse is Bijou

Millais "Mill" Crocker—Cap's boyfriend who is involved with the polo horses belonging to Teche Chartier.

Emma Crocker—Mill's younger sister.

Kitty Powell–Friend to Lockie and Cam, who is transistioning to eventing.

Teche Chartier—owns Chartier Spices "Scorching the world one mouth at a time". From Louisiana originally, Teche has a large estate nearby, one in Florida, travels on business and he enjoys life and horses.

Poppy Beck—Talia's riding student. Her pony is Tango Pirate.

Aly Beck—Poppy's mother.

Gincy Hamblett—Talia's riding student. Her pony is Beau Peep.

Annie Zakarian–new student.

Holliday "Day" Jamieson—local rider, her grandmother is the master of the Newbury Hunt. A talented artist, her horse is named Poussiere de Lune, Moon Dust and his stable name is Moonie.

Sibby Jamieson—Master of the Newbury Hounds and Day's grandmother

Buckaroo "Buck" Bouley—15 year old who wants to be an event rider

Peter Bouley—Buck's father

Greg Tolland—Victoria's farm manager, suspended for dicey financial dealings, behaving now. Tracy lives with him.

Lord and Lady Rowe–Greer's grandparents

Nicole Boisvert—Greer's junior division nemesis. Her new hunter is named Obilot.

Ellen Berlin—runs the business end of the Miry Brook Hunt Club

Mackay Berlin—Ellen's son. He's a charming financial advisor and helping organize the Miry Brook show.

Fiori "Fifi" Finzi—Jules's beautiful bad girl sister.

Betsey Harrowgate—side-saddle rider from Aside Not Astride.

Nova Reeve—college activist who interviews Greer.

Ami Gish—young summer student.

Paul Gish—Ami's father.

Annie Zakarian—new student

Ethan Monroe—the town police officer married to Sassy. Jingles is their dog.

Jingles—a Mastiff who participates in the Ambassador of Good Cheer project, Greer's charity.

Trish Meade—14 year old girl in the 4-H who trained Oliver to be the Ambassador of Good Cheer.

Oliver—rescue dog who is very cheerful

Joly—Greer's rescued pit bull puppy, who adores her

Dr. Fortier—the veterinarian

Dr. Jarosz—Lockie's medical specialist in New York City.

Mauritz Schenker—Dressage legend teaching out of Balanced Rock Farm.

Amanda Hopkins—teacher who is also helping Greer with her charity work

Bertie Warner—Greer's side saddle instructor

Sloane Radclyffe—wealthy socialite with a large farm in Pennsylvania

Ellis Ferrers—a rider at the farm briefly, and bought a horse through Cam

Jennifer Nicholson—Lockie's ex-girlfriend

Freddi—working student

Sabine—Greer's former best friend

Rui-their former train-wreck of a trainer

Gesine Hamm-Hartmann—Lockie's dressage trainer in Germany.

ACKNOWLEDGEMENTS

Thank you to Gretchen Jelinek for the use of her lovely photo of Pippa

Thank you, also, to the terrific photographer Diana Hadsall for generously making that photo available.

About the Author

Barbara got her first horse, Country Squire, when she was eleven years old and considers herself lucky to have spent at least as much time on him as she did in the dirt. Over the years, she showed in equitation classes, hunter classes, went on hunter paces, taught horseback riding at her stable and went fox hunting on an Appaloosa who would jump anything. With her Dutch Warmblood, Barbara began eventing and again found herself on a horse with great patience and who definitely taught her everything important she knows about horses. She now lives with Zig Zag, a Thoroughbred-Oldenburg mare.

Made in the USA
Middletown, DE
02 February 2016